"I've been think
all day," Trey murmured

He gently teased at her nipple through her silk blouse.

Libby thought back to the night they'd spent together twelve years ago, to the trust he'd broken. If she let him touch her again, then she'd be doomed to suffer that humiliation all over again.

"Please don't do this to me," she begged.

"What is this, Libby? Just because you deny the desire between us, it isn't going to go away." Trey took her face between his hands and kissed her. "I was there in your bed the other night," he murmured against her mouth. "I know what I made you feel."

She drew a ragged breath and backed out of his embrace. "That was lust," Libby said, her voice thin and tight. "One night was enough."

He stared into her eyes, as if searching her soul for answers. "One night every twelve years? Hell, if that's all I can hope for, then I guess I'll see you in another twelve." Then he turned and walked out.

Dear Reader,

I've traveled back to the South for the setting of my newest Harlequin Temptation novel, *Hot & Bothered*. And while you might be reading this book on a warm summer day, it was written in the midst of a snowy Wisconsin winter.

Trey Marbury and Libby Parrish are caught in both a meteorological heat wave and a heat wave of their own making in the fictional town of Belfort, South Carolina. Those of you familiar with the Low Country might recognize the real town that Belfort is based upon, although I'm not sure that a real Southern town would have quite so many charming and eccentric characters living within its limits. Or maybe it would. Maybe that's exactly what I love so much about the South.

In any case, I hope you enjoy the ideas Trey and Libby come up with to beat the heat....

Happy reading,

Kate Hoffmann

Books by Kate Hoffmann

HARLEQUIN TEMPTATION
795—ALL THROUGH THE NIGHT
821—MR. RIGHT NOW
847—THE MIGHTY QUINNS: CONNOR
851—THE MIGHTY QUINNS: DYLAN
855—THE MIGHTY QUINNS: BRENDAN
933—THE MIGHTY QUINNS: LIAM
937—THE MIGHTY QUINNS: BRIAN
941—THE MIGHTY QUINNS: SEAN
963—LEGALLY MINE

KATE HOFFMANN

HOT & BOTHERED

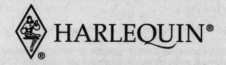

HARLEQUIN®

TORONTO • NEW YORK • LONDON
AMSTERDAM • PARIS • SYDNEY • HAMBURG
STOCKHOLM • ATHENS • TOKYO • MILAN • MADRID
PRAGUE • WARSAW • BUDAPEST • AUCKLAND

ISBN 0-373-69188-2

HOT & BOTHERED

⌐ U.S.A.

Prologue

A BUMBLEBEE BUZZED in lazy circles around a potted jasmine, the sound breaking the silence of the oppressive midday heat. A few steps away on the wide veranda of the house on Charles Street, the Throckmorton sisters stirred the heavy afternoon air with rice-paper fans. A silver tray rested on the table between their two wicker chairs, holding a pitcher of iced tea and two sweaty glasses.

"We're doomed," Eulalie Throckmorton said, her fan fluttering like the wings of a hummingbird.

Eudora Throckmorton took in the morose expression on her twin sister's face and sighed. "It's just the heat, Lalie. When I'm drenched in perspiration, I don't feel like chatting. Neither do the rest of the ladies of the Thursday Ladies' Bridge and Luncheon Club."

"But it was as quiet as a Quaker wake."

Eudora shifted in her chair. "If you'd just agree to install air-conditionin' in the house, then we wouldn't have this problem. Grace Rose Alston just had air-conditionin' put in her house and she says it's been a godsend with this mid-summer heat."

"We don't need air-conditionin', Dora. We have this lovely veranda. Mama and Papa lived here for over fifty years and they never had air-conditionin'.

Besides, we'd just shut ourselves up in the house and never see our neighbors strolling by. Out here, we're part of the world. Good gracious, if I wanted to live in the cool and dark, I'd run down to Wilbur Varner's funeral home, buy myself a nice coffin and move in next to Mama and Papa at the cemetery."

"There's no need to get all dramatic about it," Eudora replied. "I swear, you've always had a way of pilin' on the agony. You should have taken up a career on the stage. You could have given that *Driving Miss Daisy* lady a run for her money."

"And you should be sellin' gadgets on the Home Shopping Network, with your fondness for new-fangled inventions. Need I remind you that we have an electric juicer sittin' in our kitchen that you've never even used?"

"Air-conditionin' is not a new-fangled invention," Eudora countered. "Some would argue it's a necessity in the heat of a South Carolina summer. And we are approachin' an age where personal comfort is all we can look forward to on a good day."

"Let's be honest, Dora. It isn't our lack of a temperature-controlled environment that will spell the end of our beloved bridge club. It's the shortage of decent gossip. There's just nothin' left to talk about in this backwater town!"

The Thursday Ladies' Bridge and Luncheon Club was nearly a century old. Founded by Eulalie and Eudora's grandmother and a group of her friends, members were all prominent socialites in the town of Belfort, South Carolina. The club was a Belfort institution that had weathered two World Wars, Prohibition, the Great Depression and an attempted seditious coup by several members who wanted to replace the bridge games with gin rummy. But through it all, the ladies had always shared lively conversation among the sixteen members. Eulalie might call it gossip, but Eudora preferred to think of it as…illuminating discourse.

"Maybe we should consider bringin' in some new members," Eudora suggested. "Some ladies who might have some interestin' topics to share. I met a lovely widow at the Winn-Dixie who just moved from New York City."

"The ladies would never tolerate a Yankee." Eulalie shook her head. "Besides, we've always had sixteen members and until one of our ladies goes to her great reward, we can't bring in a new member. It's in our bylaws, and you should know our bylaws since you've served as president twice!"

"According to Charlotte Villiers, she herself is circlin' the drain as we speak," Eudora muttered. "If I have to listen to one more recitation of her medical woes, I do believe I might just get great-granddaddy's dueling pistol from the gun cabinet and kill her myself."

Eulalie chuckled, her mood lifting at her sister's audacious remarks. Still, this was serious business. If the bridge club struggled under her watch as president, the ladies might find some way to put the blame on her. "It wouldn't have to be anything major," she murmured. "Just somethin' juicy. Perhaps a nice political scandal would spice things up. Bribery, blackmail, corruption. Or even better, a scandal of the—" she lowered her voice to a whisper "—*private* kind, if you catch my meanin'. You know, I always believed Desmond Whitley was a homosexual. Maybe we could convince him that this would be a nice time to come out of the woodshed."

"That's closet, sister. Come out of the closet."

"Closet, woodshed. Now that would be something worth talking about."

"I like Desmond," Eudora said. "And to tell the honest truth, I don't much care if he is a homosexual. He does lovely flower arrangements for the fall bazaar at the church and he embroidered that tablecloth for the Friends of the Library auction. And he's a very fine dancer."

"All right," Eulalie grumbled. "Forget Desmond. Besides, he's sixty-two. We need to find someone younger. All the better, someone who has a spotless reputation, someone who is a stranger to scandal." She paused. "Someone who actually might participate in passionate…unbridled…slightly kinky…" She paused again, this time fanning herself frantically. "Well, I'm sure you understand what I'm gettin' at."

"Sex," Eudora said plainly. "You're speakin' of sex, sister. Good gracious, I may be eighty-three years old, but I'm a modern woman and I'm not afraid to talk about these matters out loud. Even though we're both considered maiden ladies, you and I have some experience with men. It's no use pretendin' we've never even seen the one-eyed monster."

Eulalie nearly choked on her iced tea and a fierce blush warmed her cheeks. She snatched up a linen napkin and pressed it to her lips, then cleared her throat. "There is no need for such plain speakin', Eudora."

Her sister shrugged. "You blush when I use proper

medical terminology and you blush when I choose a euphemism."

"The point I'm makin' is that despite our experience, we're still innocent to the ways of the modern world. Things have changed a bit since we were young women. Back then, a boy couldn't lay a hand on a girl's bosom without a proposal of marriage. It takes a lot more to get folks talkin' these days."

"This is silly, Lalie. We can't *make* a scandal happen. They just do."

A slow smile broke across Eulalie's face. "But we can help it along a bit."

"And how will you accomplish that?"

"Rumor, innuendo, baseless accusations. I'll think of somethin'."

"And just who will you get to participate in your little scandal?"

Eulalie slowly fanned herself. "I don't know. Someone with an upstandin' reputation." She stared at the house across the street, its wide verandas lined with hanging baskets of fuchsias. "That will take careful consideration. But one thing I can guarantee you, sister. There'll be a lot more to talk about in Belfort after I'm done stirrin' the pot. And our precious bridge club will be safe for another hundred years."

1

EVERYTHING IN BELFORT moved a little slower in the heat of summer. Dogs didn't pull at their leashes; birds retreated to the cooling shade of the live oak trees. Even the sunset took a lazy route to the horizon. Trey Marbury wiped a trickle of sweat from his neck as he waited at one of Belfort's three stoplights, grateful that night had finally fallen on a stiflingly hot day.

He peered out the windshield of his Jeep at storefronts that had once been so familiar. Sam Harrington's hardware store had a new neon sign in the front window and Royal Farley had added fancy new pumps at the filling station. But beyond that, everything was pretty much as he'd left it that day he'd driven out of Belfort, South Carolina, for the last time.

"No parade, no Welcome Home banners, no marching band," Trey muttered, turning onto Center Street. So far, the return of Belfort's former favorite son had caused little notice.

Twelve years ago, Trey had been an all-conference quarterback, homecoming king, an honor student, and had won a football scholarship to Georgia Tech—all in one year. Belfort had expected great things from Clayton Marbury III, but not nearly what his father had demanded from his only child. Clayton Marbury II wanted nothing short of perfection—and unquestioning obedience.

Trey had been relieved when he tore up his shoulder in his junior year at Tech. The pressure was off, the expectations gone. He and his father had nothing more to fight about, except the surgery that Trey refused to have and the disinterest he had shown in the family business.

In the end, that's what had brought him back to Belfort, back to his past—unfinished business. Home was no longer this sleepy little town in the Carolina low country, but a high-rise condo on the Gold Coast of Chicago. He'd lived in the north for so long he'd grown accustomed to the cold winters and the fast pace. The deep drawl that had marked his speech when he had arrived in the Windy City was nearly gone, along with his tolerance for summer weather so hot it made a man's fingernails sweat.

Trey swung the Jeep onto River Street and pulled into the parking lot of Garland Van Pelt's convenience store. He ignored the curious stares from the small group of men gathered around a television set as he walked inside. He pulled a six-pack from the cooler, then he grabbed a package of pretzels and headed to the counter.

"Trey Marbury?"

Trey glanced up from his wallet to find the storeowner staring at him. "Hey there, Garland. How's it going?" He frowned inwardly. His drawl had suddenly reappeared, each word of his greeting sliding into the next.

"Well, well," Garland crowed, clapping his hands. "Look who we have here, boys. It's Trey Marbury. We were just talkin' about you last week. About that game against Marshall. You remember that? You dropped back, Bobby Ray Talbert threw that block and you hurled the ball down the field. It bounced off the defender's back and into Lanny Freemann's arms. Belfort wins by three." The group of men erupted in a cheer, giving each other high fives.

"That was a great game," Trey said as he tossed a twenty on the counter.

"What are you doin' back in town?"

"I'm taking care of a few things for my father's estate."

The men dropped silent and Garland nodded soberly. "I heard about your dad. I'm real sorry, Trey. He was a good man."

Trey forced a smile. To most people in town, Clayton Marbury *was* a good guy, the picture of an upstanding citizen and model family man. He just hadn't been a loving father to his son. In truth, Trey couldn't remember his father ever showing an ounce of affection toward him. "Thanks," he murmured. Trey pushed the money closer to Garland, hoping to make a quick exit.

"He weren't no cheapwad, either. I never met a more generous guy. Told the funniest stories down at the lodge and could make a mean barbecue. Always threw that big shindig every year on his birthday. Yep, he looked out for his friends, he did."

"And made life miserable for his enemies," Trey added.

Garland chuckled. "You're right about that, son. Though there hasn't been much to the feud since Wade Parrish and his wife moved out of town three years ago. I think that took all the fight out of your dad. He and your ma left for their place in Arkansas a few months later." Garland totaled the price of the beer and pretzels, then dropped them both in a bag. "So how long you plannin' on stayin' here in Belfort?"

"My mother asked if I'd liquidate the last of the real estate around here and in Charleston. I've got to meet with Realtors, get some repairs made to some of the properties. I guess I'll be here for a few months at least. Just until everything closes. Then I'm headed back home. I mean, back to Chicago."

Garland nodded. "You got a place here in town?"

"The motor lodge out on Highway 32, though it took a bit of sweet-talking since I have my dog with me. I'm thinking of buying a place and renovating it in my free time. You guys know of any properties I could pick up quick?"

Garland chuckled. "Boy, the apple don't fall far from the tree. You're just like your daddy, boy! Clay Marbury was always on the lookout for a good buy. He had the Midas touch, he did."

Trey had heard just about enough about the great Clayton Marbury II. He grabbed the bag and nodded, a tight smile pasted on his face. "Thanks, Garland. Be seeing you boys."

The storekeeper scratched his chin. "Now that I think of it, the old Sawyer place is goin' up for sale. They moved Mrs. Sawyer to an old folks' home up in Florence, where her daughter lives. The house is fallin' down, so I reckon you could get a good price for it. My daughter's a real estate agent. I'll have her give you a call."

Trey waved at Garland as he counted out his change. "Keep it," he said. "Buy the boys a beer on me."

As Trey backed the Jeep out of the parking lot, he knew it would be a matter of minutes before all the town gossips knew that he was back in Belfort. No doubt, there'd be all kinds of speculation about where he'd been and what he'd been doing these past twelve years. "I should have taken a place in Charleston." He sighed. "Maybe it's true—you can't go home again."

Trey swung the Jeep back onto Center Street and headed for the old residential section of town. Belfort sat at the junction of two rivers, rivers that emptied into the Atlantic about fifteen miles downstream. Most of the huge white clapboard homes were located on the wide peninsula of land that split the rivers in two, set on streets shaded by centuries-old live oaks and boasting huge lots that backed up on the water.

Trey knew where the Sawyer house was located and headed down Charles Street. As he pulled up in front of it, his gaze drifted to the house next door. This had always been considered Parrish territory, the east side of the historic district. Since the War Between the States, Parrish supporters had lived east of Hamilton Street and Marbury supporters lived west of the dividing line. A person declared their allegiance by where they chose to buy their home. Trey chuckled softly. Buying in enemy territory would have sent his father into an apoplectic fit.

Trey reached over and grabbed a beer, then popped it open and took a long sip. Even if there were still Parrishes living in the house next door, the feud was over now. As the only Marbury heir, he had no intention of continuing the hostilities. And to his recollection, there was only one Parrish heir left and that was Lisbeth Parrish; she'd probably taken off for parts unknown at her first available opportunity.

He hopped out of the Jeep and strolled up to the Sawyer house, the facade looming darkly among the overgrown bushes and trees. Like the house next door, it boasted wide verandas that circled all four sides on both stories, shading the house from the relentless summer sun. He could see the place was badly in need of paint, and the verandas were sagging in spots. But even if it were falling apart inside, a guy didn't come across a house like this every day. The craftsmanship was incredible, the detailing probably untouched since it had been built in the mid-1800s.

Trey wiped his hand over a dusty window and tried to see inside, making out an old carved mantel and furniture covered with sheets. Suddenly, he'd found a reason to set up housekeeping in Belfort. Smiling, Trey turned back to the street. Hell, he didn't care what they wanted for the house—he'd pay it. After eight years designing everything from shopping centers to condo complexes, it would be fun to wield a hammer and saw again.

Halfway to his Jeep, Trey turned around. There had always been a secret path around the back of the old Sawyer house, a path that he and his buddies had taken numerous times on a hot summer night. It led through a dense thicket of trees and kudzu to a tiny inlet in the river, a deep pool with a sandy bottom. The high school had built a swimming pool the year after he'd graduated and the spot probably had been

long forgotten. A swim might be nice before he
headed back to the motel.

He retrieved the rest of the six-pack from the Jeep
and then walked past the empty house into the deep
backyard. Crickets chirped and unseen night animals rustled as he searched for the entrance to the
path. Though the inlet required trespassing on Parrish property, that had never stopped Trey and his
friends. If they didn't get too loud and cleaned up
after themselves, they usually went undetected.

As he pushed through the brush, Trey recalled one
time when he had been caught, and not by old man
Parrish. His memories of that night, just a few days
before his eighteenth birthday, were still strangely
vivid, for they had represented a turning point in his
life. Maybe it had been the setting or the events leading up to the encounter. Or maybe it had been his unbidden reaction that had burned the memory so
deeply into his mind.

It had been his last night in Belfort before leaving
for summer football practice at Tech. He'd started
the evening embroiled in an argument with his father, who had insisted he'd pay nothing for Trey's ed-
ucation. Though Clayton Marbury II had been born
into wealth, he had somehow gotten the idea that his
son would benefit from working his way through
college. At the time, Trey wasn't sure how he'd be
able to juggle football, architecture courses and a job,
but he'd seen the advantage of being completely free
of his father's control.

He'd stormed out, ready to find a cold six-pack
and some buddies to drink it with. But in the end, he
had decided to spend his last night alone, away from

all the big talk about athletic accomplishments and his bright future in college football. In a few days, he'd be considered a man. It was time to start acting like one.

He'd found himself at the inlet, angry and over-whelmed, confused about the direction his life was taking and scared that he might not be able to cope. She'd appeared sometime between his third and fourth beer and, at first, Trey had thought he might be hallucinating. But once he'd realized she wasn't just a by-product of a drunken buzz, Trey had been glad for the company.

Libby Parrish hadn't run with the in crowd at Belfort High School. Shy and bookish, she'd never stood out in the midst of prettier, more popular girls. She was also just a junior. And she was a Parrish, the only flaw that made any difference in his world. But that night, in the moonlight, she became something more to him.

The moment he saw her, he almost bolted. But then she spoke, telling him he didn't have to leave, that she wouldn't tell her father. Trey still remembered the look in her eyes, the curiosity mixed with a little bit of fear. Hell, he hadn't wanted to go home anyway, so why not? Besides, spending time with Libby Parrish was as good as thumbing his nose at his father.

Trey let the memories drift through his mind as he stepped around the last clump of bushes and walked into a small clearing. Moonlight sparkled on the river, and in the distance, a duck took flight, its wings flapping in the dark. Trey found an old log near the spot where they used to build a fire to fend off the

mosquitoes. He sat down on the ground and leaned
back against it, taking another long sip of his beer. For
the first time since he'd driven into Belfort, he felt like
he'd found a memory worth reliving.

But a moment after he settled in, Trey heard
rustling in the bushes behind him. With a soft curse,
he crawled behind the log and lay flat on his stomach, then reached over to grab the rest of the beer.
Though he hadn't minded breaking the law as a kid,
Trey was pretty much a stranger in town now and he
wasn't sure how the owner would feel about his presence on private property.

He waited, holding his breath, half expecting a
group of kids to appear. But a single figure stepped
through the bushes, a woman, her slender body outlined by a loose cotton sundress, her pale hair shin-
ing in the moonlight. She reached for the hem of her
dress and in one easy motion, pulled it over her head,
then kicked off her sandals and walked to the edge
of the water.

Trey sucked in a sharp breath, nearly choking as
he did. She wore nothing beneath the dress and the
shock of seeing a naked woman just a few feet away
made his pulse suddenly quicken. He wanted to look
away, but he couldn't. She was just about the most
beautiful thing he'd ever seen.

Her body was perfect, her limbs long and delicate,
her backside perfectly shaped. The light played over
her skin and he found himself caught by the graceful curve of her shoulders and the gentle indentation
at the small of her back. She lifted her arms and
slipped her hands beneath her hair, holding the wavy
mass off her neck. Trey shifted slightly as he felt him-

self grow hard, a crease in his jeans making the re-action a little painful.

But as he moved, his foot slipped and a stick cracked beneath him. She froze and then glanced over her shoulder, like a wild animal deciding whether to stay or flee. Her profile, illuminated by the moonlight, was instantly recognizable and Trey sank down behind the log.

"Libby Parrish," he said, her name touching his lips without a sound. Trey smiled. Such an odd symmetry to find her here on his first night back in town, when she'd been here on his last night.

As she walked into the water, Trey searched for a moment to make his escape. This was definitely not the time for a reunion, with her stark naked and him so obviously aroused.

The bushes directly behind him were thick and impossible to crawl through without making a noise. He'd have to get back to the path on his belly or just make a dash for it. But in the end, Trey decided not to leave. He rolled over on his back and stared up at the stars as he listened to Libby splash in the water.

She'd changed so much since the last time he'd seen her. She'd become a woman, more lovely than he could ever have imagined. But he still remembered the girl he'd known and with that memory came every detail of that night so long ago.

They'd talked for hours—Trey pouring out all his anger and frustration, giving voice to the insecurities that had plagued him, and Libby listening raptly, as if what he was saying were the most important thing in the world.

No one had ever taken the time to listen to what

he wanted out of life. Everyone had an image of who he was and what he was supposed to become. Trey had expended so much energy trying to please his parents, his teachers, his coaches and his friends, that he had wondered whether any part of his life truly belonged to him.

The night had closed in around them and Trey had felt almost desperate to stay with her for just a little longer, certain that talking with her would solve all his problems. He hadn't meant to kiss her, but it had seemed like such a natural thing. And when she'd returned the kiss, he'd felt as if the weight of the world had been lifted off his shoulders.

After that, everything had moved so quickly. She'd unbuttoned his shirt and then skimmed her fingers over his naked chest. And though the night had been hot and humid, Trey remembered shivering, all the heat in his body leaving his limbs to pool in his lap. Until then, he'd considered himself a ladies' man by high school standards, smooth and confident in the rather limited experience he'd had with willing partners.

Trey had wanted to stop, but he couldn't deny the need he'd felt with Libby. He'd longed for something more intimate, something to give him the courage to face his future. He'd found it that night in her body, in her soft touch and in the sweet taste of her mouth—in the way she'd moved beneath him.

It had been twelve years and he'd made love to plenty of women since Libby. But he still searched for that unexplainable connection they'd found, still sought a woman who combined guileless innocence with unrestrained passion, a woman who could capture his body and his soul. Though Libby had been a virgin that night, she'd been the one with the power to seduce, daring him to make love to her, soothing his doubts with her lips and her fingers.

And when it had been over and they'd dressed, he'd walked her to the path, her delicate hand tucked in his. She'd smiled at him, as if they'd shared a special secret that they'd both relive again and again after he was gone. And then he'd made her memorize his address at school and told her to write to him; he promised that he'd come home again. And that had been the last he'd seen or heard of Libby— until tonight.

Trey rolled back onto his stomach and looked over the log. Libby slowly walked to the shore, the soft moonlight gleaming on her wet skin. If he thought she was beautiful from the back, he was unprepared for the view from the front. He remembered a famous painting he'd seen on a vacation to Italy— Venus rising naked from a river. He couldn't remember the artist or where he'd seen it, but he was living it right now.

Water dripped from her hair, sluicing over her body, her skin slick. His fingers clenched involuntarily as he imagined what it would be like to touch her again. God, she was beautiful—not skinny and gawky as she'd been all those years ago. Libby Parrish had grown into a woman who could steal the breath from his lungs and make him ache with desire.

She picked up the dress and slipped it back over her naked body, then stepped into her sandals. Drawing a deep breath, she took one last look at the river before heading back to the path. Trey fought the urge to call out to her, to make the moment last longer. There were so many questions he needed answered— why hadn't she written to him, why hadn't she responded to his letters, had she come to regret the night they'd spent together? He watched as she disappeared from view, then groaned softly.

Great. Now he'd have this image swimming around in his head for the rest of the night! Especially since he was going to spend the night alone, with only his dog for company, trapped in a motel room on the edge of town. A motel room where the only distraction was an old television. An old television that got only one channel—the church channel.

Not even twenty-four-hour religion would banish his sinful thoughts or erase the image of a naked Libby Parrish from his mind. There was only one thing to do, besides leaving town at sunrise and never setting foot in Belfort again.

He'd just have to buy the house next door and find out exactly what kind of woman Libby Parrish had become.

"WOULD YOU PLEASE get away from that window?" Libby Parrish grabbed a handful of biscuit dough, took aim and hit the back of Sarah Cantrell's head.

The dough plopped onto the floor and Sarah turned around, rubbing her head. "Aren't you in the least bit curious? He's lived over there for a week. Don't tell me you haven't done a little spying of your own."

Libby sighed as she dumped the biscuit dough onto the floured counter. Sarah had been her best friend since the seventh grade, but there were times when she was an outright pain in the ass. And now that they worked together, that fact was made apparent on a daily basis. "Of course I'm not interested. Why would I have the slightest interest in what that man is doing?" She tried to add a good dose of disdain to "that man," but she only came out sounding like a prissy old woman. "Now, let's get back to this biscuit recipe. I'm concerned about the directions for working with the dough. Kneading is the wrong word to use here, especially if my readers take it in the context of bread. Kneading will make the dough too tough and—"

"He's mowing his lawn," Sarah said in her lazy drawl. "In a pair of baggy cargo shorts that are just barely hanging on to those nice slender hips of his. Oh, my, how I do wish he'd bend over and—"

"Stop it!" Libby cried, her heart skipping a beat. She drew a deep breath and tried to quash the fluttery feelings in her stomach.

"He's also neglected to put on his shirt, naughty boy." Sarah turned and grinned at her friend. "Now, I consider myself a connoisseur when it comes to the male form and I wouldn't mind taking a taste of what Trey Marbury has to offer. There was talk back in the day about how he was quite…confident with the ladies."

"Enough!" Libby shouted. She hurried to the window and grabbed the lace curtain from Sarah's fingers, dragging it back into place over the kitchen window. The very last thing Libby needed rattling around her head was talk about Trey Marbury's sexual prowess. She'd experienced that firsthand.

Her friend arched her eyebrow at Libby. "You're blushing. Why, after all these years, does Trey Marbury still have the power to get you all hot and bothered?"

"I'm not hot," Libby muttered. "Just bothered. And you know exactly why."

"Because he had the high nerve to move in next door to you? You and the Throckmorton sisters have been complaining about the falling-down condition of that house for three years now. You should be happy someone has moved in and started fixing it up."

"You know that's not why I'm bothered," Libby said.

Sarah's eyes rolled up and she groaned. "Oh, please, must we talk about that silly feud again? It's over. His daddy's passed on, your daddy's moved to Palm Beach and the rest of us in this sleepy little town have all but forgotten why the feud ever started in the first place."

"I'm not talking about the feud." Libby paused. "I can't believe you don't remember. It was only the most humiliating experience in my young life."

"Oh, the kiss heard 'round the world." Sarah grinned. "The kiss that changed your life. The kiss that—"

"I am holding a rolling pin," Libby warned. "And in my experienced hands, it could be considered a lethal weapon."

"You threw yourself at him and he couldn't resist your charms. Then he left town, never to be heard from again."

"And then, I was stupid enough to write him a letter and profess my adoration for him. Not just a few pages of 'Hi, how are you?', but a ten-page dissertation on my feelings. I actually thought we were the modern-day equivalent of Romeo and Juliet." Libby moaned. "Oh, God, I quoted Shakespeare and Elizabeth Barrett Browning."

"You never told me about the letter," Sarah said.

"He never wrote back. And he never came back to Belfort. I hear he spent his vacations working construction in Atlanta. He was probably too terrified to set foot in the town where I was living."

"It was just a kiss. A high school kiss. How good could it have been?"

Libby felt her cheeks warm. She'd been carrying the secret around for so long. Maybe it was time to tell Sarah. "It was more than a kiss. I lost my virginity to Trey Marbury that night."

Sarah gasped. "What? You and Trey Marbury—wait a second. How come you never told me this?"

"I wanted to. But after it happened I needed to think about it for a while. And then, when he didn't write back, I was embarrassed. I never was very confident with the boys and that certainly didn't help."

"And now you blame Trey Marbury for your lack of a social life?"

"No," Libby said. "I blame my busy career and living in a small town and the lack of eligible men in Belfort."

"Your career? Honey, you're every man's wet dream. You're beautiful, you make a lot of money *and* you cook. All that's missing is a short career as a stripper."

"Oh, right. Just the other day I saw a bunch of handsome single guys hanging out watching Julia Child. They were all saying how she was really hot and they wished they could see her naked." She slowly shook her head and sighed. "Sometimes I wonder how I ended up with this life. Why didn't I ever get out of this town? I'm living in my parents' old house, I spend my days stirring and slicing and sautéing. My idea of an exciting evening is writing grocery lists and reading old cookbooks. When did I turn into my mother?"

"Why *didn't* you get out of town?" Sarah asked.

Libby shrugged. "This is going to sound pathetic but I guess I always hoped he'd come back someday. At least that's what kept me here during college. And now, I have this house and I feel safe here." She sighed. "Maybe I should move. I could buy a place in Charleston and get out of Belfort for good."

Sarah watched Libby from across the kitchen, her expression filled with concern. "Or maybe you ought to just face him and put the past in the past. Bake some cookies, wander over into his yard and reintroduce yourself to your new neighbor." Sarah crossed the kitchen and grabbed Libby's hand, dragging her to the window. "Look at that," she ordered. "If you still want that man, you'd better make a move, because every other single woman in town is eyeing him up. Including me."

Suddenly, Libby didn't care about her biscuit recipe. She pushed the curtain aside and searched the yard for the subject of their discussion. "Why did he have to buy the house next door? It's like he just wanted to get under my skin."

"He probably doesn't even remember you live here," Sarah said.

"Believe me, he knows I live here. And I think that's why he bought the house. I—" Suddenly, Trey

Marbury came back into view and her words died in her throat. Libby held her breath as she watched him walk the length of the side lawn. Sweat glistened on his bare chest and his finely muscled arms strained against the push mower. As he passed, her gaze didn't waver. His dark hair clung damply to the nape of his neck and Libby's eyes dropped lower, to the small of his back, revealed by the low-riding shorts. Sarah had been right. If his shorts dropped any lower, she'd enjoy a full appreciation of his backside.

He turned and started back in the opposite direction, Libby's gaze now taking in a deeply tanned torso, marked by paler skin above the waist of his shorts and a line of hair that ran from his belly to beneath the faded fabric. She lingered over the view for a moment longer, then realized she'd forgotten to breathe. "He's changed," she murmured.

"It's been twelve years," Sarah said as she began to gather up her papers from the table. "We've all changed."

Libby looked over her shoulder with a rueful expression. "I guess we have." But Trey Marbury had become a man in those years, a man who seemed to exude power and strength, even in the simple act of mowing his lawn. Libby swallowed hard, memories of their night together flooding her brain.

A girl's first experience was supposed to be awkward and painful. But that wasn't how Libby remembered it. He'd been so gentle and sweet to her, taking her places she'd never been before. Libby couldn't help but wonder what twelve years had done to his abilities in the bedroom.

"I wonder why he came back," Libby murmured.

"He's not really back," Sarah replied. "Wanda Van Pelt sold him the house and she says that he's taking care of his daddy's business concerns in the area and just renovating the house as an investment. He's been living in Chicago and has some big career up there." Sarah turned away from the window and wandered over to the recipes they had spread across the table, finally resigned to getting back to the job at hand.

"He probably doesn't even remember the letter you sent him," Sarah murmured. "And you could use a few more male prospects besides Carlisle Whitby, Bobby Ray Talbert and Wiley Boone."

"Carlisle is my mailman," Libby said. "And Bobby Ray is our police chief. And I barely know Wiley Boone."

"He's the city building inspector and Flora down at the drugstore says that Wiley was inquiring about you the other day. I think he plans to ask you out. And Carlisle always gives you the extra coupon flyers and he hangs around on your porch after he delivers your mail, just hoping you'll come outside. And Bobby Ray asks you out every New Year's Eve and every Fourth of July, regular as clockwork. So which would you prefer—one of those three besotted fools or Trey Marbury?" She raised her eyebrow. "Or maybe you want to end up like the Throckmorton sisters?"

"I'm not going to be a spinster!" Libby said. "I could have a man in my life—if I wanted one. I just haven't found the right one."

"Now you've got four to pick from."

"That's some choice," she murmured.

"Well, I'm off," Sarah said, gathering up her things. "Like panties on prom night."

Libby chuckled softly. "I'll try the biscuit recipe tonight and see how the cheese variation turns out."

"You could try bits of sausage or bacon as a variation, too."

Libby turned back to the window. "Fine. Bacon sounds good." She heard the front door close; her gaze was firmly fixed on the man who lived next door. Clayton Marbury the third. He'd been Trey for as along as Libby could remember, the only son of Clayton and Helene Marbury. At one time, the Marburys had owned the bank, the general store, a string of gas stations, two car dealerships, the newspaper and half the commercial properties on Center Street. The Parrish family had owned the other half, a fact that only added fuel to the conflict over which family was the most powerful in Belfort.

Had any other single, handsome man moved in next door, Libby might have been happy. After all, it had been five years since the humiliation of her last boyfriend's infidelity, five years since she'd had a serious relationship with a man. But Trey Marbury? Every instinct told her to stay away.

Libby closed her eyes, then slipped her hands beneath her hair and lifted the pale blond strands off her neck. This heat wave was setting her nerves on edge. And the fact that she was almost a month late with her newest cookbook wasn't helping matters. In another week, she'd begin taping the next season of *Southern Comforts,* the PBS cooking show she'd been doing for the past two years. The book had to be printed and ready to ship when the first show aired in January, or she'd lose sales and viewers.

"So get to work," Libby muttered, letting her hair

drop back onto her shoulders. "And stop thinking about the past. You were a silly lovesick girl living out a fantasy that was never supposed to be real. And he was nothing more than a one-night stand." She took a last look out the window and then froze, her fingers clutching the lace of the curtain.

Trey Marbury was no longer cutting the grass. He now stood in the side yard chatting with Sarah Cantrell! Libby's mouth dropped open as she watched her best friend flirt with the enemy. They seemed to be caught up in a lively exchange, laughing and joking with each other. When Sarah reached out and brushed her hand along Trey's biceps, Libby ground her teeth. "Traitor," she muttered beneath her breath.

Libby's fingers twitched as she tried to imagine the sensation of touching him…smooth skin, slicked with sweat, hard muscle rippling beneath. She hadn't touched a man in so long that she'd nearly forgotten what it felt like to run her palms over long limbs, to sink against a male body and to be enveloped in a strong embrace. He was tall, well over six feet, with wide shoulders and a narrow waist—not a trace of the boy was left in him.

Why had he always fascinated her so? From the time she'd first known who Trey Marbury was, her parents had warned her against him. There'd be no socializing with the enemy. It wasn't difficult, considering she and Trey ran with different crowds—Trey with the popular kids, and Libby with those who preferred the library to football games and Saturday night dances.

It wasn't until she began noticing the opposite sex that Libby realized how dangerous Trey really was.

Just looking at him made her think of things that her mother had warned her about—meeting boys beneath the bleachers before school, kissing in the balcony at the movie theater, doing unspeakable things in the back seats of cars. Whenever Libby had thought about these things, the boy in her head had always been Trey and the girl he'd chosen to seduce had been her.

As she peered through the window, an unbidden rush of jealousy and a warm flood of desire collided deep inside of her. Desperate to know what Sarah and Trey were talking about, Libby tried to read their lips. But the attempt brought only frustration. She'd need to get closer. If she just wandered out to the veranda to water her hanging baskets, she might be able to overhear their conversation.

Libby grabbed her watering can from beside the back door and tiptoed to the side veranda, but all she could hear was the indistinct murmur of voices—and laughter, lots of laughter. Sarah had always been more comfortable around men, but this was ridiculous! This wasn't just a friendly conversation anymore—Sarah was flirting!

She'd have to get closer. Drawing a deep breath, she headed toward the steps and then crept along the line of azalea bushes that created a hedge between the two properties. The voices got louder and when she finally settled between two rose bushes, she could hear everything Sarah was saying.

"I'm sure she'll stop by soon," Sarah said. "She's been very busy, what with the book and the show. She starts taping the new season in the next few weeks. Have you ever seen her show?"

"I can't say that I have," Trey replied. "I've been living in Chicago."

"Oh, we're on the PBS station in Chicago."

"You're on the show, too?" Trey asked.

"No, I produce the show. And I help Libby edit her cookbooks and test her recipes."

A rustling in the azaleas drew Libby's attention away from the conversation. She nearly screamed when a wet nose poked through a hole in the bushes. Libby gave the golden retriever a gentle shove and wriggled back a few inches.

"Is that your dog?" Sarah asked. "You better not let him in Libby's yard. She is pathological about her roses. Her grandma planted those roses years ago and Libby treats them like her children."

Trey whistled softly. "Come here, Beau. Come on, boy. He's been chasing squirrels all day. You can take the dog out of the city, but you can't take the city out of the dog."

"Go," Libby whispered, waving her hand in the dog's face. "Get out of here, you mangy mutt!" But Beau took her frantic movements as encouragement and he leapt through the bushes and knocked Libby flat on her back. Libby flailed her arms as the dog stood above her and licked her face with his cold tongue, his muddy paws planted firmly on her chest. Libby closed her eyes and covered her face with her hands.

When the dog finally stopped, she risked a look up to find both Trey and Sarah staring down at her. An amused grin quirked Trey's lips.

He chuckled softly. "Well, well, well. If it isn't Lisbeth Parrish."

"I—I have to go now," Sarah said, forcing a smile.

"I've got recipes to type. I'll call you later, Lib. Nice seeing you again, Trey. Y'all take care now."

"Oh, we will be talking," Libby muttered, pushing up on her elbows and brushing her hair out of her eyes.

Trey grinned, his arms crossed over his bare chest. "I was wondering when you were going to stop by and welcome me to the neighborhood." He held out his hand to her, but Libby slapped it away, humiliated that she'd been caught spying on him.

"Is that any way to welcome me to the neighborhood? Where's my chicken casserole and my pineapple upside-down cake?"

Libby struggled to get to her feet, the roses scratching at her arms and face. He found this all so amusing. Probably as amusing as he'd found her letter, full of flowery prose and professions of love. "I only bake casseroles for people I'm happy to see."

"Lisbeth, I expected a much more hospitable welcome."

Biting back a curse, Libby brushed the mud off her cotton sundress. "I may have to tolerate your presence next door, but I don't have to like it, *Clayton*. You're a Marbury and I'm a Parrish. What do you expect from me beyond hostility?"

Trey frowned and for a moment, Libby regretted her sharp words. This was not the way she wanted to begin, but he seemed to delight in her embarrassment. He took a step toward her and she backed away, but he managed to capture her chin.

"Stay still." He slowly turned her head, then ran his thumb along her cheek.

"What—what are you doing?"

"You're bleeding," Trey said. He reached down

and withdrew a bandanna from the pocket of his shorts. Gently, he dabbed at her cheek. "You shouldn't lurk in the roses. They have thorns."

Libby stared up at his face, unable to drag her gaze away. He was much more handsome than she remembered—but then, she remembered him as a boy, a high school football star with a disarming smile and a body worthy of a Greek god. He was a man now, and his features had a harder edge; his mouth was firmer and his jaw stronger. She felt her heartbeat quicken and suddenly, she couldn't breathe.

"I—I wasn't lurking."

His gaze met hers directly and she saw eyes so blue they sent shivers down her spine. When he licked his upper lip, Libby lapsed into contemplation of how his tongue might feel moving across her mouth, tracing a path along her neck, dipping a bit lower. She swallowed hard. Why was this happening to her? She'd had other men in her life—handsome, attentive men. But they'd never made her feel this way, all light-headed and breathless, as if she were teetering on the edge of something very dangerous.

"It doesn't look too bad," he said, leaning closer to examine her wounds. "Shouldn't leave a scar."

"I suppose I should thank you," Libby said as she drew away. "But since your dog was the cause of my accident, I don't think I will."

He stared at her for a long moment, as if he could read her mind, and then shrugged. "Just trying to be neighborly."

Libby brushed the dirt off her dress. "With a line like that, it's a good thing we're standing in my garden," she muttered. "My roses need the fertilizer."

Trey hitched his hands up on his waist and shook his head. "Maybe you ought to just lay back down with the rest of the prickly things in this garden, Lisbeth."

The insult stung. She hadn't meant to act so nasty, but Trey had a way of making her feel like a seventeen-year-old geek all over again. "So we finally see the real Trey Marbury," Libby murmured, crossing her arms beneath her breasts and straightening her spine.

"What is that supposed to mean?"

She tipped up her chin. "Tell me, of all the houses in Belfort, why did you choose to move into this one?"

"You think I bought this house because of you?" Trey chuckled. "Now don't you have a low eye for a high fence."

Libby ground her teeth. He looked so satisfied, as if he had her exactly where he wanted her! All the confidence he'd possessed as a teenager had increased tenfold and Libby knew he'd have a snappy retort for anything she might throw his way. Well, she wasn't a girl anymore. She was a woman fully capable of defending herself against his charms. "You're no better than any other Marbury, all of you crooked as a barrel of snakes."

"So that's how it's going to be?" Trey asked, taking a step toward her, his eyes glittering with amusement, goading her.

"Just stay out of my way," Libby warned. "Keep your dog out of my garden and keep your nose out of my business. I'm watching you."

"Yes, I know. I've seen you peering out from behind those starched curtains. For someone who values her privacy, you're just a little too interested in your neighbors. Or is it just me you find so fascinating?"

Libby took a step forward, standing so close to him she could feel the heat of his body. She poked him in the chest, setting him back on his heels. "Don't dare presume that I have even the slightest interest in you, Marbury."

His jaw went tight as he stared into her eyes. Then, in one quick movement, he grabbed her hand and swept it behind her back, pulling her body up against his. At first, she was too stunned to protest. And then, when she opened her mouth to speak, all she could manage was a tiny gasp.

Libby's eyes drifted down to his lips and she wondered if he had any intention of kissing her. If he did, she wasn't sure that she'd be able to do anything about it—except perhaps kiss him back. But when her eyes met his again, Libby's heart froze. It was there, in the icy blue depths. He knew exactly what she was thinking.

Trey's lips curled into a grin and he chuckled softly. "What? Can't think of anything to say?"

"What I have to say to you isn't fit for civilized ears."

He leaned closer to her, taking his own sweet time as he did. Libby waited, frantically wracking her brain for some acidic comeback or well-aimed put-down, certain he was about to kiss her and knowing she didn't want to stop him. But before his lips touched hers, he paused, hovering so close she could feel his breath on her face.

Her heart hammered in her chest and Libby felt herself losing touch with reality. All she could think about was this moment and how everything hinged on her reaction. She didn't move, barely breathed, her body trembling with anticipation.

And then, he did it. She knew it was coming, but she still wasn't prepared for the flood of desire that raced through her bloodstream. In single fleeting moment, his lips were on hers. A tiny moan slipped from her throat as she collapsed against him, and he took it as an invitation. His tongue slowly traced along her bottom lip and then invaded, taking possession of both her mouth and her ability to reason.

Every nerve in her body seemed to come alive, every thought focused on the feel of his lips on hers. She'd kissed a small number of boys in her life, but this wasn't just a kiss. It was a challenge, a dare, the first salvo in a battle that had just begun—and Libby couldn't show any weakness. They weren't kids anymore and along the way, they'd acquired some very adult weapons.

She returned the kiss in full measure, her tongue meeting his, touching and tangling until the taste of him filled her. Her hands flitted to his face and then furrowed through his hair, tempting him to surrender and declare her the victor.

When he finally drew away, Libby looked up at him, proud of her effort. She expected to see the self-satisfied grin she'd come to know, but instead he appeared to be as consumed by the kiss as she was. He gazed down at her through half-hooded eyes, and his breathing was shallow and quick.

"I think we've gotten off to a fine start," he murmured, allowing his nose to bump against hers. "In fact, I think I'm going to enjoy the neighborhood just fine."

With that, he let go of her arm. Libby stumbled back, light-headed and weak-kneed, nearly falling into the rose bushes again. But she caught herself just in time, straightening her posture and smoothing her trembling hands over the front of her dress. "Don't be so sure. Just because you managed to kiss me doesn't mean I've changed my mind about you."

"*Managed* to kiss you? Considering your response, I more than managed. Besides, if you think there was anything romantic about that kiss, you're wrong."

"Really?" Libby said. "Why did you kiss me then?"

"It was the only way to keep you from hurling another insult at me," Trey replied.

"Well, there's a much easier way to accomplish that. You could just run on down to the train tracks and take yourself a nice long nap." She glanced at her watch. "The train comes through at about three, so why don't you plan on sleeping 'til four?"

"I don't think I'll be doing that," Trey said.

"Then just stay out of my life. Keep your dog out of my garden and your face out of my line of vision and we'll get on just fine. And if you're going to do yard work, at least wear a shirt."

"My, I have missed that Southern hospitality." He slowly backed away. "Just warms a man's heart."

Libby ground her teeth. There was no winning with him, no getting the last word! Deciding it was best to cut her losses, she turned on her heel and started for the house.

"I'm looking forward to that cake, Parrish."

Libby clenched her fingers into fists. "No more than I'm looking forward to the day when you lose your testicles in a tragic lawn mower accident, Marbury," she shouted over her shoulder.

As she continued her retreat to the house, Libby smiled to herself. Maybe she had gotten the last word. It wasn't the most poetic turn of phrase, but the imagery had certainly hit the mark. Yet, there was no satisfaction in the victory. Though she might have won the battle, Libby wasn't looking forward to waging the war.

It was entirely too difficult to remember that Trey Marbury was the enemy—and that falling for him again would mean surrendering the last shreds of dignity she had left.

2

TREY SEARCHED THROUGH the darkened room for his drill bits, the heat in the second-story bedroom making it hard to breathe. Since he'd moved in, he'd been sleeping on an old sofa downstairs, the tall windows thrown open to catch even the slightest breeze.

Hell, he'd been living up north for so long that he'd forgotten what a South Carolina summer was like—the unrelenting humidity, so thick it made everything stick to the skin, including whatever clothes a person could stand to wear.

It was easier to work inside once the sun went down, and there was plenty of work to do. The old Sawyer house had been left to ruin three years ago; its elderly owner had been reluctant to sell after she'd moved to a nursing home. It had been on the market just a few days when Trey moved back to Belfort and he'd jumped at the chance to buy it, offering a cash deal to speed up the sale. He'd moved in before the deal closed, ready to begin the renovations.

He'd told himself that the work would take the place of a social life in town. But after his encounter with Libby three days ago, Trey had been forced to reexamine his motives for choosing to buy this particular house.

Over the years, he'd thought about Libby, about their night at the river. No matter how he rationalized what had happened, it all still felt unfinished to him, as if there were still words that hadn't been said, feelings that hadn't been resolved.

The moment he drove into town, it was as if he were driving into the rest of his life. As much as he wanted to deny his small-town Southern roots, he'd come home, to a place where he had history. He'd come home to a place where people knew him and cared about him. Maybe he'd come back to Belfort hoping that he'd find Libby.

Trey bent down and picked through a pile of paint scrapers he'd tossed on the floor. So their first meeting hadn't gone very well. Trey hadn't expected it to be a lovefest, considering the feud that had always stood between their families. But he hadn't expected outright hostility. They'd shared an incredible night; certainly that had to have meant something.

Obviously, it hadn't. She'd never written him, never tried to make contact, even through he'd sent five or six letters. But all that had happened a lifetime ago. Libby was no longer the pale and skinny girl he knew, her wide green eyes always watching him but never meeting his gaze, taking such care to stay out of his way. She was a woman now and he was a man. Things had changed.

Trey sucked in a sharp breath. Maybe that was the way to rationalize the kiss he'd shared with her—it was just a male response to a beautiful female, purely animal in its origins. But Trey had never acted on impulse when it came to women. Every move in his romantic life had come after careful consideration. But what he felt for Libby Parrish had nothing to do with romance.

Trey snatched up the plastic case that held his drill bits and then straightened. He'd been thinking about Libby all afternoon and evening, trying to figure out what it was that had caused him to temporarily lose his mind. Yes, he was attracted to her, but at the same time, he knew to keep a safe distance. Trey was already the subject of rampant speculation around town and the last thing he wanted was to add a woman—especially Libby Parrish—to the mix of rumor and gossip. If he wanted a sex life, he'd have to find it in Savannah or Charleston, not next door.

Crossing the room to the window, Trey vowed to put every last thought of her out of his head—to forget the sweet taste of her, the feel of her body against his. But when he pushed aside the dusty drapes to open the window, he found himself faced with something more than just a mental picture. The bedroom window looked right out on Libby's bedroom, now ablaze with light. He stepped back and let the motheaten curtain drop, but his curiosity got the better of him. Hell, if she could spy on him, he could certainly return the favor.

He parted the drapes again and watched. It was obvious she wasn't aware of the view he had, or maybe the house had been empty for so long that it had never been a concern. Three tall windows spanned the width of her bedroom and opened onto the second-floor veranda. She hadn't bothered to pull the lace curtains that hung on either side.

Trey watched her make the bed, shaking out freshly laundered sheets and smoothing them over the mattress of the huge four-poster. She wore a simple cotton dress, loose and flowing, like the one she'd worn that night at the river. The fabric clung to her body and outlined long slender legs and a tiny waist. The neckline was cut just low enough and gaped slightly when she bent over the bed. But Trey was left to fill in the image with memories of their kiss, his hand sliding along her back and then around to her hip, her breasts pressed against his naked chest.

She walked to the window and Trey fought the impulse to step away. He knew the room was dark and that he couldn't be seen. Libby slowly unbuttoned the front of her dress, then turned and lifted her hair from her neck, letting the meager breeze cool her. Trey gnawed on his lower lip, suddenly wondering if she knew he was there, if every move was meant to taunt him further.

With a soft curse, he turned away from the window. He'd do well to find some feminine companionship and find it fast. Fantasizing about Libby Parrish was an exercise in masochism. She'd made her feelings about him patently clear—there was no love lost between the Parrishes and the Marburys, and there'd be none to find between him and Libby.

Trey tucked the drill bits into his back pocket and headed downstairs. Beau was waiting for him, his leash in his mouth and his tail thumping on the floor. "No way," Trey murmured to the golden retriever. "We're not going for a walk now. Nighttime is work time." The dog trotted after him into the kitchen where Trey grabbed a cold beer from the refrigerator. He popped the top and then took a long drink, tipping his head back to let the ice-cold liquid slide down his throat.

The interior of the house was a wreck, the result of his enthusiastic demolition. The kitchen was the only thing he hadn't touched. A guy had to eat, though he hadn't been doing much of that lately. Chicago was known for great restaurants and he'd been spoiled, never taking the time to cook for himself. But Belfort had a much more limited selection, though the restaurants served good Southern home cooking.

"What I wouldn't do for some decent Thai food," he muttered, his stomach growling. As he took another sip of his beer, Trey's cell phone rang. He picked it up from the kitchen table. "Trey Marbury," he said.

"When the hell are you coming back to Chicago?"

He immediately recognized the voice of his business partner. The day to day stress of running a successful real estate development company seemed to result in an edgy, almost frantic tone for Mark Callahan and Trey knew that this was a phone call he wasn't anxious to take. "Hey, Mark. What's up?"

"This isn't going to work."

"It hasn't even been two weeks," Trey said. "That's barely a standard vacation. Besides, I spoke with Dave this morning. If there are any problems, he's promised to call me. I can always drive back for a day or two if necessary."

"Listen, when you said you had to leave for a couple of months, I figured you'd be gone a couple of days. You're not actually going to stay away for two months, are you?"

"I need some time," Trey said. "I've got a lot of crap to sort out. When my father died in May, I came down here for the funeral and left the same day. I'm not sure I really dealt with what was going on. I need to do that now. Besides, isn't this one of the benefits of being a partner?"

"Can't you deal with your crap up here? We've got really good psychologists in Chicago."

"No, it's got to be here. I've got to take care of some things for his estate and I bought a house that I'm renovating."

Mark gasped. "You bought a house?"

"Yeah, you ought to see this place. It was built in the mid-1800s and it's got all the original architectural detailing. It's going to be sweet when it's finished. I'm doing a lot of the work myself. I was going to flip it, but I'm thinking I might just keep it for a vacation home."

"It sounds to me like you're planning to stay a lot longer than two months," Mark said.

"Well, I'm not. Now, was there a specific problem you called to discuss, or can I get back to work?" They chatted for a few more minutes, Trey reassuring his partner that he was not abandoning the business. When he finally got off the phone, Beau was still sitting at the back door, his tail thumping. Trey tossed the phone on the table and then let the dog out. But to his dismay, Beau made a beeline for the azalea hedge. "Ah, hell," he muttered, shaking his head.

Running after the dog, he got to the bushes just as the golden retriever scampered through a hole. Trey whistled softly and called, but the dog had never been very obedient. Had it been any other backyard, Trey would have walked away and let the dog wander. But he didn't need Libby Parrish banging on his door at sunrise to complain about the condition of her roses.

The grass was cool and damp beneath his bare feet as he circled around the hedge and walked into Libby's garden. As he came around the back corner of the house, he saw Beau sitting on the back porch, his nose pressed against the screen door.

"Get over here!" Trey hissed. "Beau! Come."

The dog glanced over at his master, but refused to follow orders. Trey started toward the back door, but then a figure appeared in the doorway and he froze.

She had changed from her dress to a gauzy nightgown that left her arms and shoulders bare. Her hair had been pulled up and twisted into a knot, but damp tendrils brushed her temples and curled against her neck. At that moment, Trey was certain that he'd never seen anything quite as beautiful as Libby Parrish. The light from the kitchen outlined her slender form and created a shimmering halo around her body. She looked like an angel, pure and unapproachable.

"What are you doing here?" she asked.

For a moment, Trey thought she was talking to him, but then he realized she was speaking to Beau. He waited, unwilling to break the silence of the night, hoping that the dog would turn and run.

Libby glanced both ways, then pushed the screen door open. "Are you lost? You live over there, not here." She reached down and patted the dog on the head. Trey winced. Beau was an easy mark. The slightest show of affection turned the dog into a loyal friend. It would take ten pounds of raw steak to get Beau to leave now.

"Are you hungry?" Libby asked. Beau wagged his

tail and stood up, nuzzling her hand. "Wait here," she said. "Stay. Sit."

Libby disappeared into the house and returned a moment later with a plate of biscuits. The smell drifted through the air and Trey groaned softly. He hadn't eaten anything since lunch and the scent made his mouth water. He watched as Libby plucked a biscuit off the plate and held it up for the dog.

Beau jumped up and snatched it out of her fingers, gulping the treat down in one bite. "You like that?" she asked. "Bacon bits. Here, try this one. It's got cheddar cheese and bits of jalapeño." The dog gobbled down the second offering without even chewing. "You're hungry. Doesn't anyone feed you over there? Good dog. Try this one. It's got little bits of sausage in it. Very savory."

The light from the house shone behind her and every time she shifted, the fabric of her nightgown became virtually transparent. His image of an angel disappeared and instead, Trey saw a temptress, nearly naked to his eyes. He knew he ought to feel guilty for keeping to the shadows, yet he couldn't seem to bring himself to announce his presence.

His gaze drifted up from her bare feet, along her legs, to her belly and the dark triangle just below. She wore nothing beneath the nightgown and as his eyes moved up, he could see the soft curve of her breasts and the deeper pink of her nipples.

Trey felt himself growing hard, his body as stimulated as his mind had become. What was this instant desire he felt and why couldn't he control it? Trey took a step back, ready to make a safe escape. But the minute he moved, Beau pricked up his ears and trotted down the steps.

To Trey's dismay, Libby followed. He stepped out of the shadows and Libby jumped in surprise. "I'm sorry," he said. "I didn't mean to scare you. He ran over here before I could stop him."

Libby stared at him for a long moment, as if trying to decide whether to speak or just walk back inside. "You don't scare me," she murmured, shrugging her shoulders.

"Sorry," Trey repeated, keeping his eyes fixed on her face and hoping his shorts were baggy enough to hide the growing bulge. "It smells good out here."

"I'm testing biscuit recipes," Libby said.

Trey forced a smile, fighting an urge to cross the distance between them and kiss her again. Only this time, the kiss would be gentle and seductive. "It's been a long time since I've had a decent biscuit. Up north, they eat toast and English muffins for breakfast."

"And try to find good grits," she said. "Well, that's impossible."

Trey nodded, remembering the intoxicating taste of her mouth. "Although they make decent hash browns at this place on Division and—well, never mind." He wasn't even sure what he was talking about, only that it was keeping his mind from thoughts of running his hands over every inch of Libby's body. Trey cleared his throat. "I'll just take my dog and you can get back to your biscuits."

"Would you like some?" Libby asked. "I have extra."

The offer took him by surprise, an unexpected truce he didn't want to rebuff. It wasn't a kiss, but it was a step in the right direction. "Sure."

"I'll just go get some." She hurried back into the

house and returned a moment later with a small basket. She'd taken the time to line it with a checkered napkin before stacking the biscuits neatly inside.

Trey slowly approached her and took the basket from her outstretched arms, his fingers brushing against hers. The contact sent a frisson of heat through his arm. "Thanks. They smell great."

"Try one," she urged.

He smiled, cocking his eyebrow up. "You didn't happen to slip a little rat poison in these, did you?"

"No," she said, sending him a playful glare. "But I can whip up another batch in a few minutes if you like."

Trey grabbed a biscuit and bit into it. "Oh, God," he murmured as the biscuit melted on his tongue. The outside was golden brown and flaky, and inside, it was still warm. "This is the best biscuit I've ever eaten. You know, these are almost better than—" Trey paused and cleared his throat.

"What?" Libby asked.

"Nothing."

"No, really. Be honest."

Trey shook his head. "I was going to say they were better than…sex."

This brought a tiny smile to her lips. "Bad food and bad women. Is that the real reason you decided to leave Chicago?"

"I'm glad I'm home," Trey said, his gaze meeting hers.

They stared at each other for a long time, neither one of them moving or speaking. He fought the urge to pull her into his arms again and test the limits of their attraction. Would she welcome another kiss?

Did she even realize how much he wanted her? Crazy thoughts raced through his head, fantasies that involved more than just a kiss. Trey glanced down at Beau, looking for anything to take his mind off the woman standing in front of him. "Well, thanks for the biscuits." He held the basket out to her.

"No, take them with you. You can bring the basket back later."

"Great," Trey said. He reached down and grabbed Beau's collar, tugging him along after him. "And I'll make sure he doesn't get in your yard. High fences make good neighbors, right?"

"Right," she said. "Good night."

He glanced over his shoulder. "Good night... Libby." Using her first name seemed almost too intimate, but Trey was past caring. All this treading carefully was making him crazy. Without another thought he let go of Beau's collar and dropped the basket on the grass. In a few long strides, Trey crossed the distance between them.

Taking her face in his hands, he kissed her, his mouth covering hers, his tongue gently teasing. When he finally drew away, he looked down into her face. Her eyes were closed and a tiny smile curled her lips. "There," he murmured. "That's better."

Her eyes fluttered open and she drew a shaky breath. "Th-that thing I said about the lawn mower accident? I didn't really mean it."

Trey chuckled. "Yes, you did. But I won't hold it against you." He slowly walked back to Beau and grabbed the dog's collar again, then picked up the basket. "I'll see you around, Libby."

"See ya," she called.

THE ELECTRIC FAN whirred on Libby's bedside table but did nothing to dispel the heat in her bedroom. She lay unmoving on the bed, her arms and legs splayed, the sheets tossed aside. She thought about turning on the old air conditioner, but it made so much noise that she'd never get to sleep. And sleep would be her only relief from the thoughts that plagued her mind.

A tiny breeze fluttered at the curtains and Libby sighed softly, then rolled onto her stomach. She'd been trying to sleep for nearly three hours and was just a few minutes short of giving up completely.

"Damn him," she muttered, punching her pillow. "Damn that Trey Marbury."

Libby was loath to admit what had been keeping her awake, but that didn't stop her mind from wandering into inappropriate territory—namely Marburyland. From the moment he'd moved in next door, she'd vowed to maintain her distance. It had taken her years to get over him the first time and she wasn't going to go through that again.

She touched her lips as she remembered how it felt to kiss him. There had been times in the past when she'd thought back to the night they spent at the river, the passion they'd shared. But a simple kiss in the here and now was enough to make all those memories pale in comparison.

A shiver skittered down her spine. If only the moment had been repugnant or disgusting, then maybe she wouldn't be faced with a long night spent thinking about Trey. But the way he had pulled her into his embrace, the way he'd taken possession of her mouth and shattered her resistance…she wanted to hate him for the power he held over her, but instead, Libby was drawn to him, intrigued by desire she couldn't control.

She rolled over again and closed her eyes, but the images wouldn't go away, and this time, they didn't stop with just a kiss. Libby imagined his hands on her body, brushing aside her nightgown, searching for bare skin. He'd cup her breast, smooth his thumb over her nipple and tease it to a peak.

A tiny moan slipped from her throat as desire twisted at her core. His touch wouldn't be gentle or tentative. He'd know how to make her ache, how to make her shiver and writhe. And when his fingers weren't enough, he'd use his tongue and his lips to drive her wild.

Libby rubbed her stomach with her palm, tempted to satisfy the ache herself simply to get Trey Marbury out of her head. It wasn't him she wanted, Libby rationalized. She'd just been without a man for such a long time…it was about pure desire. It had nothing to do with how he made her feel.

With a low curse, Libby clenched her fists and pounded them into her pillow. He wasn't going to make her want him again. Tomorrow morning, she'd wake up and she'd forget he lived next door. She'd go on about her life without reliving the kisses they'd shared, without rewinding their conversations.

Libby rolled off the bed and walked out to the hall. French doors opened from the hallway onto the back veranda and she wandered over to them. From there, she could see the back part of Trey's house as well as his yard. The house was still ablaze with light and she wondered if he was having as much trouble sleeping as she was.

As she stared out into the quiet night, Libby ran her fingertip along her lower lip. "So he's a good kisser," she murmured. "He's probably had a lot of practice." But even thinking about all the women he'd had since that long-ago night didn't alleviate the desire.

Her mind flashed an image of him, naked, lying in her bed, fully aroused. She swallowed and tried to put the picture out of her head, but it was slowly burning into her brain, a spot of intense light that wouldn't disappear even when she closed her eyes.

"Stop it!" she said, clenching her fists at her side. "This is ridiculous!" There had to be a way to put an end to this fascination, to make sure neither one of them ever crossed that line again. But how could she bring up the subject in conversation, especially since she'd vowed to stay away from him?

"I'll write him a letter," Libby murmured.

She turned and hurried down the stairs to her office. Her desk was stacked with vintage Southern cookbooks and sheets of hand-written recipes. Libby reached out to turn on her computer, but decided a personal note would be best. She grabbed several sheets of her personalized stationery and then picked out her favorite fountain pen before wandering back upstairs to her bedroom.

Libby sat down in the overstuffed chintz chair near the window and fanned herself with the stationery as she considered what to write. "I should outline my expectations," she murmured. "We need to maintain a cordial, but neighborly relationship."

She gnawed on the cap of the pen for a long mo-

ment before she began writing. "Dear Mr. Marbury."
She shook her head. "Dear Trey?"

Dear? "Dear" seemed far too affectionate. But
what other choice was there?

"I'm writing this letter so I might address some of
the…concerns I have over our recent…" She
groaned. "I can't say 'kiss.' Our recent interactions.
Though the enmity between our two families has
been long-standing, I am hopeful that we can put
the past behind us and maintain a cordial, if not
friendly, relationship."

Libby reread the first part of the letter and nodded.
It was clear that more kissing would not be wel-
comed. "To that end, I'd like to suggest we follow a
prescribed set of guidelines when it comes to our future interactions."

The letter sounded so formal. This was a man
whose kisses made her toes tingle, a man she had a
very memorable sexual history with, a man who had
caused her heart to race and her head to spin. Why
would *any* unmarried woman want a man like that
to stay out of her life?

"Because, I'm completely insane," Libby muttered. "The gossip around town would be unbearable. And if my parents ever found out, they'd
probably kill me. And, after he goes back to Chicago,
I'll be a complete wreck. Four good reasons."

Libby wrote a few more lines, then read the letter
again. But suddenly, the idea of making rules to follow seemed childish. She picked up the paper and
crumpled it into a ball; then she began again.

There had to be a way to put her feelings into
words, to make him understand her insecurities

without admitting how long it had taken to get over him the first time. Any contact between them would only be tempting fate.

By the time she finished her fifth draft of the letter, the sun was beginning to brighten the horizon. Downstairs, the mantel clock struck five and Libby signed the letter, folded it and slipped it into an envelope. It had taken nearly three hours, but she'd managed to put her thoughts into words. Now she just had to deliver the letter.

Libby crawled out of the chair, rubbing her tired eyes with her fingertips. She grabbed her robe and slipped into it, then tucked the note in her pocket. If she snuck out under cover of darkness, she could avoid the nosy neighbors and running into Trey.

The neighborhood was quiet as she stepped outside, the sound of a blue jay's call echoing from the top of an oak tree. Libby glanced up and down the street, then hurried down the front steps and across the damp grass. All the lights were off at Trey's house and she tiptoed up to the front door. Wincing, she opened the squeaky top of the brass mailbox and shoved the letter inside. For a moment, she considered snatching it back out, but then decided that a letter was the only way to handle the situation between them.

As she ran back to her house, her feet wet with the morning dew, Libby breathed a sigh of relief. She'd done it. She'd put any possibility of a relationship with Trey firmly behind her. Now, she could finally stop spending her days and nights thinking about him.

She yanked the door open and rushed inside, then slammed it shut behind her. Her heart beat hard and she gulped in a deep breath. "Everything's going to be all right now," she whispered to herself. "Everything can get back to normal." But even as she said the words, Libby didn't believe them.

As long as Trey Marbury was living next door, nothing would ever be normal again.

TREY FROWNED as he heard the soft thud of footsteps on the front porch. Grabbing his mug of coffee, he strolled to the front door and peeked out the beveled-glass window, only to see Libby Parrish racing across his front lawn. He quickly opened the door, anxious to speak to her again. But by the time he got outside, Libby had already disappeared.

He shook his head and then glanced around. If she'd come for a reason, then she'd obviously changed her mind. The fact that he didn't find a flaming bag of dog poo on the porch or eggs splattered on the windows was a good sign. At least they'd moved past open hostility.

With a shrug, he picked up the newspaper and walked back inside. For now, he wasn't going to try to figure out what was going through Libby's mind. It was enough to know she enjoyed kissing him.

He started back to the kitchen, his stomach rumbling with hunger. Trey grabbed the orange juice from the ancient refrigerator and a box of cereal from the counter. He'd just filled a bowl of Cap'n Crunch when a knock sounded on the front door. Trey jumped up and wiped his hands on his shorts, wondering if Libby had changed her mind. But when he caught sight of his visitor, Trey frowned.

"Hello," the mailman said.

"Hi," Trey replied.

"I thought I'd take the opportunity to introduce myself, Mr. Marbury. I'm Carlisle Whitby. I'm your U.S. postal carrier. I'll be responsible for delivering your mail."

"Great," Trey said, wondering why that warranted a personal introduction.

"You probably don't remember me. We attended high school together."

"Right, Carl Whitby. You were a couple of years older, weren't you?"

"That's correct, Mr. Marbury. But I go by the name Carlisle now. It's more befitting an employee of the U.S. Postal Service. Fourteen-year veteran. Joined up after I graduated from Belfort High."

Trey rubbed the back of his neck, working out a kink from spending another night on the couch. "Is there something I can do for you, Carlisle?"

"No, but there's something I can do for you." The mailman held out a stack of mail, then pointed to an envelope on the top. "I found that in your box."

"What is it?"

"It's not a piece of stamped and postmarked mail. Postal regulations prohibit the use of a designated U.S. Postal Service mailbox for anything other than the U.S. mail. Now, I'm willing to let you go this one time, but I'd appreciate it if you'd inform whoever placed this envelope in your box that it is against federal regulations."

Trey took the mail from Carlisle and then examined the envelope in question. "I'm not sure who this is from."

Carlisle snatched the envelope back and examined it. "Looks like an invitation," he said. "A-2 envelope, linen finish. This would be one of your finer grades of stationery. Many of the ladies around town use it. Tansy Miller orders it special down at the Paper Barn."

"Thanks," Trey said, grabbing the envelope and adding it to the stack of mail.

Carlisle smiled. "I know my mail. I know my zip codes, too. Ask me any city in our fine state and I can tell you the zip code."

"I'll keep that in mind if I ever need to mail a letter," Trey said. He nodded, then quickly stepped back inside the house. When he closed the door behind him, he sighed. There were some benefits to an anonymous life in the big city. In Chicago, he'd never even met his mailman.

He tossed the stack of mail on the end table and examined the plain envelope. A floral scent drifted through the air and he touched the letter to his nose. Whoever had written it had doused it with perfume before dropping it in his mailbox.

His curiosity piqued, Trey slipped his finger under the flap and pulled out a single folded page.

I dreamt about you last night. I wasn't sure I should tell you, but the dream was so vivid, I woke up believing it was real. Did you come to me in the darkness? Did we act out some forbidden fantasy? Or was the memory of your touch merely imagined? All I remember is I wasn't surprised when you appeared in my bedroom. You didn't have to tell me why you'd come, because deep inside, I knew I willed you to that exact place in time. We didn't speak.

There was nothing to say once you kissed me. I wanted you to possess me, to own me. I felt your hands on my body, touching me, making me ache for something more. I should have told you to stop, but I didn't. And when you finally brushed aside my clothes and carried me to the bed, I was beyond all reason, desperate to feel your body above mine, inside mine. Was it a dream? And if it was, will it come again tonight?

Trey stared at the letter in disbelief. What the hell was this? He flipped the paper over, but there was nothing written on the back, no indication of whom it came from, no signature, no return address on the envelope, nothing.

"This has got to be some kind of a joke," he murmured. But as he read it over a second time, he realized it wasn't obscene enough to be a joke. Whoever wrote it knew how to spell and how to put together a sentence. The handwriting looked distinctly feminine and a bit old-fashioned and the stationery was watermarked and expensive.

"Libby," he murmured, a gasp of surprise slipping out with her name. She'd been on his porch this morning. What else could she have been doing except slipping the note in his mailbox?

"Libby Parrish, you naughty girl," Trey murmured with a chuckle. She seemed so cautious around him, as if wary of his motives. He scanned the letter again.

If he were a suspicious man, he might believe she was leading him on, simply for the chance to shut him down when the time came. She was a Parrish and he was a Marbury. And she had dumped him once before. Trey could see her taking a perverse pleasure in doing it again.

Trey shook his head. Libby had lived in Belfort her whole life; and folks in town expected her to be the picture of Southern propriety and gentility. He knew all about expectations. Maybe she just wanted to cut loose every now and then, to enjoy the pleasures of the flesh with a willing partner.

But was he a willing partner? To his eyes, Libby was just about the sexiest woman he'd ever met. Since he'd first set eyes on her again, his thoughts had been filled with images of her, his mind conjuring one fantasy after another, fantasies that usually involved the two of them naked and aroused.

Though his mind had occasionally wandered into the land of sexual fantasy, Trey hadn't made a habit of lapsing into daydreams about sex—until now. What was it about Libby that intrigued him so?

He'd had a social life in Chicago but, in retrospect, the women he'd dated and bedded had always worn their sexuality on the outside, unafraid to make their wants and needs known, almost aggressive in their pursuit of pleasure. There'd been no coy glances and hidden longings, no indecision, no pretending and certainly no erotic notes left in his mailbox. Sex had been a transaction, an exchange of mutually beneficial orgasms. In short, there'd been no mystery.

At first he'd found no-strings sex to be a welcome convenience. But he'd grown up believing that women were supposed to be capricious and unpredictable, that sex was an illicit pleasure, and that made the chase and conquest even more satisfying. How could he not be intrigued by a woman who'd take the time to put her feelings of lust into a letter?

So what the hell was he going to do about it? He could throw the note out and pretend he'd never received it. Or he could march across the lawn and demand to know why she'd sent it. Trey drew a deep breath. Or he could walk through her door tonight and do exactly what she asked. He could seduce her.

A knot of desire twisted inside of him and he groaned. He'd be the first to admit that it had been too long between sexual encounters. But was he ready to throw himself into a passionate affair with Libby? And was he ready to face what would come after that? Hot, sweaty sex between the heirs to the Marbury-Parrish feud would not go unnoticed in Belfort. And then there was the whole prospect of walking away from her again. He'd done it once before and he wasn't sure he'd be able to do it again.

Trey tossed the note onto the pile of mail, determined to put thoughts of Libby out of his mind for now. He'd wait until they ran into each other again and then decide how to proceed. He'd take careful stock of her mood, determine her motives and then make a decision.

Trey strode to the kitchen and picked up the keys to the Jeep and then noticed the empty basket sitting on the counter, still lined with the checkered napkin. He had an excuse to see her again—to return the basket and thank her for the biscuits. Perhaps he should use the opportunity to figure out what was going on in Libby's head.

As he jogged down the back steps, the humidity

nearly knocked him over. The heat wave had been relentless, making him restless and on edge with the lack of sleep. How was a guy supposed to think straight in an atmosphere that seemed to melt away all his inhibitions?

Up north, he'd grown numb to his environment, to the grating sounds of traffic and smells of a busy city. But here, everything seemed to be designed to tempt the senses—the heavy scent of flowers, the lazy songs of the birds, the rustle of a fickle breeze in the live oaks and the taste of a freshly baked biscuit. He wanted to indulge in it all, to satisfy every little desire.

Trey hopped inside the Jeep, turned the ignition and opened all the windows. The air conditioner blew out hot air and he cursed softly at the merciless weather. What he wouldn't give right now for a crisp autumn day in Chicago, with the wind blowing off the lake and the clouds drifting in front of the sun. Summer in the South could really get under a guy's skin.

Everything moved slower—people, cars, even the stoplights seemed to take their time changing. Trey headed for the drugstore; Band-Aids were the first thing on his list. He pulled into a parking spot in front and jumped out of the Jeep, smiling at a little girl sitting outside the door with a drippy Popsicle.

Harley Simpson was behind the counter when Trey walked in, the bell jangling above the door. Trey gave him a wave and Harley called out his name. "I see Tech got that quarterback from Charleston. Threw for over three hundred yards in one game. That'll never beat the game you played against Carter High where you and Frankie Jackson connected on that 98-yard touchdown in the last ten seconds. Lord, that was a sight."

"That was somethin'," Trey said, forcing a smile. The townsfolk seemed caught in a time warp, still thriving on talk of his past glory at Belfort High and Georgia Tech. He hurried to the back of the store, hoping to avoid any more dissertations on how it was a damn shame he'd wrecked his arm and how he'd have been a great NFL quarterback if it hadn't been for his injury. Trey had given up that dream years ago; the folks in Belfort were still living it.

Harley's wife was minding the pharmacy and she smiled at Trey as he plucked a box of bandages off the shelf. He turned to walk back up to the front, but paused beside a display of condoms. He stared at the colorful boxes, some promising increased pleasure, others touting better lubrication. He reached for a box of twelve, knowing that he should be prepared for any eventuality.

"Those are a top seller. You can't go wrong there."

Trey jumped at the sound of Flora Simpson's voice and glanced over his shoulder to find her standing behind him. "Thanks," he murmured.

"Although these are our second-best seller." She pointed to a blue box. "See, they have these ribs. Supposed to be good for the lady." Though Libby's pleasure was of paramount importance to Trey, he wasn't about to discuss it with Flora Simpson.

The bell above the door jangled and Trey snatched up a box of three, but Flora grabbed his arm. "That's not your best buy," she said. "This twelve-pack saves you twenty-three percent. And then we have the economy pack. Harley always says you get more bang for your buck that way." She smiled up at Trey. "So, who's the lucky lady?"

"There is no lucky lady—I mean, there isn't, yet. I just—"

"Flora, I need some boric acid. I've got these ants building hills in my rose garden and…" Her voice trailed off as Libby noticed Trey standing next to Flora. Her gaze met his and Trey smiled. Lord, she was pretty. Even though the heat wilted everything in sight, she looked so…fresh. He wanted to pull her into his arms and inhale the scent of her hair, run his hands over her smooth skin. Had Flora not been standing next to them, he would have pulled her behind the condom display and kissed her.

"Hi," Trey said.

Libby glanced between Flora and Trey. Her gaze dropped down to take in the small package in his hand. "I—I'm sorry. I didn't mean to interrupt."

"You weren't," Trey said, shoving the box back onto the rack. He held up the Band-Aids. "I just stopped by for these."

Flora watched the two of them with a suspicious eye and then smiled. "Say, Libby, I have a recipe you might like. It's for my grandmother's Brunswick stew. I'd be happy to make it on your show. I know you had the governor on last season and he did his mama's Frogmore stew. Though I've never tasted the governor's stew, I'm sure my Brunswick stew is much better and I'd—"

"I could use that boric acid," Libby said.

Flora sighed. "I've got to check in the back."

"No, that's all right," Libby said, "I'll—"

"No, no," Flora insisted. "I'll fetch it straightaway." She bustled off, leaving Trey and Libby standing in front of the condom display.

She smiled wanly. "Ever since I had Governor Winston on, everyone in town is looking for a guest spot."

Trey drew a deep breath and marshaled his thoughts. The scent of her perfume, hints of citrus and flowers, filled the air. He tried to recall the scent on the letter, but couldn't place it. "I'm glad I ran into you," Trey said, reaching out to hook her hand with his little finger. He ran his thumb over the back of her wrist.

She shifted uneasily, glancing over her shoulder to see who might be watching, her pale hair falling in careless waves around her face. He searched her gaze, looking for some sign that she'd sent him the letter, afraid she was about to bolt. But what the hell was he looking for—lust, guilt, embarrassment? Or was that part of the game she was playing, this calculated indifference? He was tempted to sweep her into his arms and kiss her, simply to gauge her reaction.

"I wanted to thank you again for the biscuits," he said. "I had the last of them for breakfast."

"Great." Another long silence descended around them and she forced a smile. "Well, I should really go. I've got a lot of work to do. Tell Flora I'll stop by for the boric acid later."

He nodded. "I'll see you, Libby."

She backed away, her smile fading slightly. "Bye, Trey."

By the time Flora returned with the box of boric acid, Trey had managed to curse himself up one side and down the other. God, Libby Parrish made him feel like a bumbling kid again! Looking into those green eyes, he could hardly put a sentence together, much less express a coherent thought.

"Where did she go?" Flora asked.

Trey shrugged. "She said she'd stop back later," he murmured. He smiled as he took the box of Band-Aids to the counter. Though Libby maintained a very proper facade in public, he knew what was bubbling beneath the surface. She was a passionate woman and tonight, he'd find out how far she was willing to go for pleasure.

3

"He was buying condoms! You know what that means, don't you?"

Sarah took a long sip of her lemonade, watching Libby over the rim of her glass. "He's a sexually responsible adult who apparently doesn't buy into that whole 'saving it for marriage' concept?"

"No," Libby countered. "It means he's planning to have sex. A man doesn't buy condoms unless he has…prospects."

"You think he has the hots for someone around town?"

"I don't know…."

Sarah's eyes popped open wide. "You think he's going to make the moves on you!" she accused.

"I do not," Libby lied. "Having sex with Trey Marbury has never once crossed my mind. It would be a stupid thing to do, especially after what happened the last time."

"I thought it was good," Sarah said.

"The sex was. But the leaving part wasn't. I'm not going to put myself through that again. I don't want him." She drew a deep breath. "I don't."

"Sell that story somewhere else," Sarah countered. "I don't believe you. If Trey walked in here right now, ripped off his clothes and offered himself to me, I'd jump his bones without a second thought."

Libby glared at her friend as she folded whipped egg whites into the custard mixture for an orange-buttermilk pie, a recipe she'd found in an old church cookbook. "I should have put that letter in his mailbox."

"What letter?"

"I wrote him a letter last night explaining how I hoped we could be friends. I put it in his mailbox, but then I had second thoughts and took it out a few hours later."

"So, you're still hot for him," Sarah said. "That doesn't surprise me. Before I left the other day, I must say, I saw some sparks between the two of you."

"And you were the one waiting on the sideline with the can of gasoline. If you hadn't talked to him, I wouldn't have fallen in the rose bushes and Trey and I wouldn't have had a blistering argument. I also wouldn't have suggested a messy lawn mower accident involving his manhood."

Sarah gasped, laughter bubbling from her throat. "You didn't."

"I did. And then to make things worse, I let him kiss me. And then, later, his dog came over and then he came over and I gave him some biscuits and…I let him kiss me again."

"Trey or the dog?" she interrupted.

Libby rolled her eyes. "Very funny. Trey. And don't look at me like that. I just happened to have some biscuits fresh out of the oven."

Sarah wagged her finger. "I've known you far too long, Libby, and that's the way it always starts. You see a guy you like, you find some way to ply him with your cooking and a few bites later, he's putty in your hands."

"Well, not this time. I was just being neighborly."

"Oh, and you kiss all your new neighbors?" Sarah grinned. "I think Trey does plan on having sex with you."

Libby paused before pouring the filling into the partially baked piecrust. "Did I invite you here tonight or did you just show up to bug me? I can't recall."

"I didn't have anything better to do on a Friday night."

The clock in the front parlor began to strike eleven and Libby wiped her hands on a dishtowel. "Go home. And take that sweet potato pie recipe with you. We've got that and the orange-buttermilk pie recipe to test and then we're done with the desserts."

"Then we're done for good," Sarah said.

"We are?"

She nodded. "I've tested everything else. This is the only thing I've been waiting for."

"The cookbook is done?" Libby murmured, her voice laced with disbelief. "It can't be done."

"We've finished everything you outlined last fall. We've tested every recipe and prepared every menu. You've written all the copy and I've proofread all the recipes."

Libby set down the mixing bowl and spatula, stunned that the year's worth of work was done. The time had passed so quickly. In just a few months, she'd be thirty years old. She frowned. Her career had consumed her life, so much that the days seemed to fly by in a haze of ingredients and manuscript pages. Last year at this time, she'd had so many plans, both professional and personal. She'd resolved to take a vacation, to meet new people, to find a nice man to date, all before her thirtieth birthday.

"What's wrong?" Sarah asked.

Libby looked up, her thoughts interrupted. "Nothing. I was just thinking how fast time passes. It seems like just yesterday that we finished the last cookbook." She paused. "I thought things would be different, that's all."

"How?"

Libby shrugged. "I don't know. I guess I was hoping something exciting would happen in my life, something major."

"Your show was picked up by seven more stations. You're about to publish your second cookbook. I'd say life is definitely looking up."

Libby grabbed the pie and bent to place it in the oven. When she straightened, Sarah was watching her with a discerning gaze. "I'm happy. I am. And I'm grateful to you. The show was your idea. I just wanted to put my family recipes in a cookbook. You're the one who made it all happen."

"Good, you should be thankful," Sarah said, giving Libby a hug. "I'm a very good friend. And as your friend, I'm going to give you a little advice. If you want something exciting to happen in your life, you're going to have to take a few risks."

Libby was about to argue but then sighed and smiled wearily at her friend, too tired to protest. "You're probably right." She rubbed her temple. "This heat is really getting to me. I think I'm going to clean up here and take a nice cool bath. Why don't we start proofing the rest of the cookbook manuscript next week? We've got to go to Charleston tomorrow to check out the new set and we can go over the menus that we have planned with the graphics people. I have some ideas there that I'd like them to try."

Sarah gathered up her things and stuffed them into her tote. "I'll pick you up tomorrow morning at ten."

Libby nodded and then followed Sarah to the front door. She watched as her friend walked to her car parked at the curb, waving as Sarah drove off. Turning back to the silent house, Libby tried to shake the melancholy that had come over her in the kitchen. She did have an exciting life. Her career was taking off, speaking engagements all over the country had given her a chance to travel and she was becoming known as an expert in low-country southern cooking. What more could she want?

When she reached the kitchen, she stood in front of the counter and groaned. "This is what my life is. Pie." Bourbon pecan pie, orange-buttermilk pie, lemon meringue pie. She'd spent her entire day baking pies in ninety-five-degree weather. "But they're excellent pies."

She'd been satisfied with her life until Trey had moved in next door. Now, she spent her time thinking about him, fantasizing about what they might share, wondering if it would be as wonderful as she imagined.

She grabbed up a towel, ready to begin cleaning up the spilt flour and dirty bowls, but then immediately tossed the towel aside. Instead, she retrieved the pitcher of lemonade from the refrigerator, poured a tall glassful and walked out to the back veranda, turning off the kitchen lights as she left.

Libby stood at the screen door, pressing the cool lemonade glass against her cheek. Her knit camisole and cotton skirt clung to her damp skin, but a tiny breeze rustled the live oaks in the backyard. She pushed at the door and walked outside, sipping the tart drink as she strolled through the yard.

The scent of roses hung in the air and the musical sound of the crickets drifted through the quiet night. In the distance, thunder rumbled and lightning flickered. Above, the moon shone through a gauzy haze. She stood in the middle of the lawn and closed her eyes, drawing a deep breath and waiting for the breeze to freshen.

Just a few minutes ago, while saying goodbye to Sarah, she'd been exhausted, spent by the heat. But now, when left alone with her thoughts, she became restless, her mind filled with images of Trey.

She wanted to put him out of her head. Yet something about the man held her in this strange limbo—he was dangerous and intriguing, maddening and exciting. She wanted to hate him, to punish him for what he'd done all those years ago. Yet he represented everything she was missing in her life.

"It's just the heat," she murmured, her eyes still closed. "If it would only rain, these feelings would go away." People had been known to go stark raving mad in the midst of a heat wave. Libby was beginning to understand why.

She opened her eyes and her breath caught in her throat. He stood ten feet away, next to the hedge, his tall frame barely visible in the dark. Libby blinked, certain that it was just a trick of the moonlight. She took a step back and he moved. It was only then that Libby realized the man standing in front of her was real, flesh and blood, and not some apparition she'd fantasized.

It was late, far later than proper for a neighborly visit. And he was barely dressed—a cotton shirt open to the waist, baggy shorts and bare feet. Her heart slammed in her chest and she prayed that he'd disappear as quickly as he'd appeared. But then he began a slow approach, his gaze fixed on her face.

For every step he took toward her, she took one backwards, unsure of what to do. She needed time to think. Time to understand what this undeniable attraction really was. When she reached the steps, she hurried inside the house and then stood at the screen door and watched him. He waited there in the moonlight, unyielding, unmoving.

With a trembling hand, she reached for the latch on the door, then drew her fingers away. Common sense warned her to run, but she was tired of running. For once, she wanted to take a risk, like she had that night twelve years ago. Libby gave the screen door a shove, opening it wide, then turned and slowly walked through the darkened house.

Her feet brushed softly over the oriental carpet on the stairs, her mind acutely aware of the sensation. All her senses seemed to be suddenly keener, taking in the cool of the wooden banister, the smell of lemon furniture polish and the sound of her heart thudding in her chest.

When she reached her room, she sat on the edge of the bed and waited. Seconds ticked by, her pulse settling into an easy rhythm. Libby closed her eyes again. Had she imagined seeing him? Was this all part of a cruel trick her mind had played?

She slowly counted to one hundred and then opened her eyes. He stood in the doorway of her bedroom, watching her again, waiting. Her mind scrambled for something to say. Why had he come? What was he expecting?

She slowly rose and opened her mouth to speak, but he shook his head and touched his finger to his lips. Then, he held out his hand, giving her the choice. She could walk into his arms and be lost forever, or she could turn away and he'd disappear. It all came down to one choice—her whole life down to this single moment, a heartbeat to make a decision that might change things forever.

Libby drew a deep breath and crossed the room. Wrapping her arms around his neck, she stared up at him. His hands moved up to cup her face and he kissed her, his tongue gently testing, then invading. She should have been surprised, but she wasn't. This was exactly what she'd been waiting for, this undeniable heat. She'd just never expected to find it again with Trey.

She had thought so much about the feel of his lips on hers, about the taste of his tongue; it was as if one hunger was being satisfied, only to have another spring to life inside her. She wanted his hands on her body, his skin touching hers.

His lips moved from her mouth to her neck. Brushing aside the strap of her camisole, he kissed her shoulder, then gently grazed the skin with his teeth. A shudder raced through her and she felt her knees wobble. All the secrets that she'd kept about that night became clear in her mind. This was what she remembered—this power to possess, this helpless hunger.

He traced a line with his tongue, from her shoulder, along the curve of her neck to the base of her throat, then lower. And when her top stopped his descent, he reached down and grabbed the hem. In one motion, he pulled it up and over her head.

His mouth found hers again and he furrowed his fingers through her hair as he kissed her. The taste of Trey was intoxicating, melting the last shreds of her resistance. Libby's breasts pressed against his naked chest, her nipples hard with the contact against damp skin.

She'd formulated so many fantasies involving Trey over the past few days, but the experience of his touch was so much more than she'd ever imagined. His fingertips were electric on her body, his lips a fiery brand. She wasn't a girl and he wasn't a boy anymore. They were both adults now and they knew what they wanted.

His hand slipped down to caress her breast, his thumb teasing her nipple. Her sigh sounded loud to her ears and she realized that they hadn't said a word. The seduction was unfolding in silence. But there were no words for what she was feeling, this inexorable climb toward her release. Every touch drew her closer and closer, and Libby was suddenly afraid of the power he held over her. She'd kept such tight control over her life. Could she allow herself this vulnerability?

Libby drew back, staring up into his eyes, but she could barely see his face in the feeble moonlight that filtered through the windows. He kissed her again, deeply, then scooped her up and carried her towards the bed.

As Trey set her back on her feet, he reached around for the button of her skirt and a moment later, the thin cotton garment was pooled on the floor. His shirt followed before he gently pushed her back and they tumbled onto the bed together.

Outside, thunder rumbled and the wind shifted direction, blowing at the lace curtains and whistling through the screens. The storm inside her body raged even more violently as she lost herself in Trey's seduction. His hands and lips and tongue danced over her sweat-slicked skin. She should have wanted to stop him, but everything inside her ached for more of the same.

Trey rolled to her side and she caught sight of his face in a flash of lightning. His expression was intense, his brow furrowed. Libby reached up and smoothed her hand across his forehead and then along his beard-roughened cheek. It had been so easy to hate Trey, but the reasons didn't make sense anymore, especially when he made her feel so…alive.

His lips found her breast and Libby sank back into the mattress, arching as he teased at her nipple with his tongue. When he finished, he moved lower, kiss by kiss, trailing a damp line to her belly. She sucked in a sharp breath, her body beginning to tremble, her mind losing touch with reality.

And then he was there, first with his fingers, sending wild waves of sensation through her body. Libby cried out as he slipped a finger inside of her. She didn't need to think. Her mind automatically focused on his touch, sure and determined, yet incredibly gentle. And when his tongue found the nub of her desire, spasms rocked her body.

Libby writhed on the bed as he played out her orgasm, begging for him to stop the torment yet unable to control the shudders that raced through her. It seemed to go on forever, further evidence of his power over her. And though she felt at her most vulnerable, something inside of her sensed that she could trust him with this.

He brought her down slowly; her breath came in tiny gasps, her hands twisted through his hair. And when he moved back beside her, his lean body brushed along hers, sending a fresh wave of desire to her core.

Trey nuzzled the curve of her neck, his face still damp with her release. She closed her eyes and listened as the storm rolled through, crashing all around them. And when the rain began and Trey got up to close the windows, Libby closed her eyes, relieved that it was finally over—the heat wave, the longing inside her, the anger and regret she'd carried for so long. They all seemed to be one and the same.

She drifted off, exhaustion overwhelming her, and when Libby opened her eyes to the pale dawn, he was gone. It hadn't been a dream. Her body still tingled where he'd touched her and the scent of him still hung in the air. She was past trying to figure out what made her want him. Desire was unpredictable and sometimes undeniable.

And for now, that was explanation enough.

EUDORA THROCKMORTON SAT primly on the edge of the sofa, watching her sister sleep. It was nearly ten in the morning and Eulalie was normally up with the chickens. She also preferred to sleep in her own bed, not in their mama's favorite Chippendale chair pulled up next to the front parlor window.

"Sister!" she whispered. "Sister, wake up!"

Eulalie's eyes popped open and the field glasses she'd been holding landed on the carpet with a soft thud. "Good Lord, what time is it?"

"Ten in the morning. Did you fall asleep here? When I went up to bed, you said you'd be right along."

A tiny smiled twitched at the corners of Eulalie's mouth. "It worked. As sure as rain when there's clothes on the line, my plan has worked."

"What plan?"

"My plan to create a little scandal in Belfort. It worked. Last night, due to my efforts, Lisbeth Parrish and our new neighbor, Clayton Marbury, had a secret assignation. I do believe they might have had—" she lowered her voice "—intimate relations."

"Great day in the mornin', what are you babblin' on about? Have you gone completely 'round the bend?"

"I've come to believe that it was Providence that brought Mr. Marbury to buy the Sawyer house. Imagine Parrishes and Marburys living right next door to each other. And that Clayton is such a handsome young fellow. And Lisbeth, a lovely girl, but flirtin' with spinsterhood. It was bound to happen. I just helped it along a bit."

"Let me get you a cup of tea, sister. I believe you've become delusional. I'm going to call Dr. Lassiter."

Eulalie grabbed Eudora's hand before she had a chance to escape. "I'm in full possession of my faculties, Dora, and the picture of good health."

Eudora clutched at her sister's hand. "Then explain what this is all about."

"I placed a letter in Mr. Marbury's mailbox yesterday. A very...erotic letter suggestin' that a certain lady wanted him to pay her a visit. Of course, I didn't use names. I let Mr. Marbury believe what he would. I watched the house all day and all night and—well, let us just say, when you have a rooster, he's bound to crow."

"You told me you were watchin' birds with Papa's field glasses but I don't believe roosters are found in Mr. Audubon's *Guide to Birds*."

"Back to the point, I saw Clayton Marbury leaving the Parrish house at two in the mornin'. And he wasn't wearin' his shirt or his shoes. How do you think Belfort is going to react to that little bit of scandal?"

Eudora shook her head. "There is just no chance of a Marbury and a Parrish falling into an illicit affair. Her father would be furious and his daddy would turn over in his grave. I can't believe you'd countenance that! Libby Parrish is our second cousin twice removed, and we owe a loyalty to her. We have Parrish blood runnin' through our veins."

"Oh, please, sister, everyone is long past carin' about that feud." Eulalie snatched up the field glasses from the carpet and peered out the window. "There she is! Waterin' her fuchsias. She has a glow about her this morning." She stood up. "I'm going to go have a chat with her. See if I might be able to ascertain a bit of factual information from her."

"Don't you dare," Eudora warned, reaching out. "I won't have you stirrin' up trouble."

Eulalie slapped at her sister's restraining hand.

"I'll be able to tell exactly what happened. I have a very fine eye for these things."

Eudora had no choice but to follow her sister outside. Whatever had prompted this ridiculous behavior would have to be nipped directly in the bud. The Throckmorton sisters had a reputation to maintain in Belfort. Resorting to scandal-mongering would be unacceptable.

"You are not going to spread lies about these two young people," Eudora said. "I won't allow it."

"Hush, now," Eulalie said as she hurried across the street. "Lisbeth! Lisbeth, dear. I must speak with you."

The sisters bustled up the front walk of the Parrish home and greeted Lisbeth with cheery waves. Eudora studied their neighbor carefully and was surprised to notice a rather remarkable change in her appearance. Her complexion looked rosier, her green eyes brighter, and a tiny, self-satisfied smile touched her lips.

"We just had to come over and see how you were doin', dear," Eulalie continued. "After this unfortunate turn of events, we've had you in our prayers."

"Unfortunate?"

"The Sawyer house," Eulalie said. "The nerve of that man, buying property right next door to yours. Like a slap in the face, don't you think? Those Marburys are no better than trash."

Libby sent Eulalie an uneasy smile. "I'm sure Trey Marbury has the right to buy a house anywhere he wants."

Eudora frowned. Perhaps her sister was correct. For a Parrish to show tolerance to a Marbury was unheard of in Belfort. "Has he spoken to you?"

A tiny blush crept up Lisbeth's cheeks. "Of course. We have a very cordial and neighborly relationship. That silly feud is in the past. I think it's time it came to an end, don't you? Besides, I don't even remember what it was all about."

"Oh, I know," Eudora chirped up. "Your families have been fighting since the War Between the States. His great-great-great-grandfather accused your great-great-great-grandmother of sympathizing with the North. Your great-great-great-grandfather called him out and they had a duel right in the middle of Charles Street. Lucius Marbury shot Edmund Parrish in the back."

"More like the backside," Eulalie said. "The way Mama told it, after Edmund took a wild shot and missed, he decided that he didn't feel like dyin' on that particular day so he took off like a rabbit out of a hole."

"That's not how it went, sister."

Lisbeth held up her hand. "I'm sorry. I really have to be going now. I have to drive to Charleston today. But I'm grateful for your concern."

The sisters watched her hurry up the front steps and disappear inside the house. Eulalie turned to Eudora and smiled. "Can there be any doubt, Dora?"

Eudora clutched her sister's arm. "I don't believe there can be. Lisbeth Parrish looks like she enjoyed the company of a man last night. And I do believe that man was Clayton Marbury III."

"Come, sister," Eulalie said, pulling Eudora back across the street. "We have another letter to write. Only this time, it will be addressed to the young lady. Now, I'm concerned about the theme of this letter. It was quite simple to write the first since it contained a lady's sensibilities. But how are we to choose words that might come from the mind of man?"

"They are complex creatures," Eudora mused. "But when it comes to sex, I believe they're all pretty much the same, dear. Perhaps we might have to do some research. Harley Simpson carries some of those men's magazines down at the drugstore. They must be quite racy since he has to wrap them in brown paper before he puts them out on the shelves."

"*Playhouse*," Eulalie said.

"*Playboy*," Eudora corrected. "The problem is, I'm not so sure that our buyin' a men's magazine might not just stir up more gossip than the gossip we're tryin' to create."

"Then we'll just have to take a little road trip, Dora. There's a lovely adult bookstore out on the interstate. I'm sure they'll have what we're lookin' for."

"Good idea," Eudora said. "I've always wondered what would cause a man to just stop what he's doin' to visit a store like that. Now I'll know."

LIBBY STARED OUT the window as Sarah pulled the car off the highway and headed into Belfort. The sun had set over an hour ago, calling an end to an exhausting day of production planning for the next season of *Southern Comforts*. Charleston had been caught in the grip of the same heat wave, but the studio had been an air-conditioned oasis.

"You really like the set?" Sarah asked.

Libby nodded. "Sure. It's great. It's very nice."

Sarah glanced over at her, a concerned frown wrinkling her brow. "Come on, Lib. What's wrong?

You always have strong opinions on these matters. You've been walking around in a fog all day. Give me a little feedback."

"I've just got a lot to think about."

"*I'm* supposed to think about all the problems with the set and the taping schedule and the lighting. I'm the producer."

"Right," Libby said, forcing a smile. In truth, her thoughts had been firmly in the realm of her personal life, not her professional life. Though she'd managed to escape Trey's presence for an entire day, she hadn't been able to keep him out of her head.

Warmth flooded her cheeks as memories of the previous night filled her thoughts. Every instinct told her that she'd made a mistake, that making love to Trey would just draw her back into all the pain she'd experienced twelve years ago. Libby wanted to believe she'd grown past that, but had she? The desire she'd felt last night had been more powerful than anything she'd ever experienced before. It wasn't something she could just forget once Trey left town. "This heat is making me crazy," she murmured.

"I thought we'd finally get some relief last night," Sarah commented. "But it just seemed to get hotter after that storm."

"I hate the heat," Libby said, slumping down into her seat and turning the air-conditioning vents toward her. "I should just move. Go north, where the summers are at least tolerable."

"What is causing this mood of yours? And if you say Trey Marbury, I'm going to pull this car over and slap the silly out of you."

"Please do," Libby said. "It might help."

"All right, do I have to guess, or are you going to tell me?"

Libby closed her eyes and tipped her head back. "You'll never guess. Even I don't believe it."

"You kissed him again," Sarah said, her words blunt and matter-of-fact.

Libby chuckled softly. "If only I'd stopped there. But that was just the start of it."

"Oh, Lib, I was just kidding about the kiss. Don't tell me you threw yourself at him again."

"Nope. This time, he threw himself at me. He just appeared last night, right before the storm hit and one thing led to another and we…"

"Wait!" Sarah commanded. She pulled the car over to the curb and turned her full attention to Libby. "Did you have sex with him?"

Libby pressed her hands to her flaming cheeks. "We didn't actually have sex, but we did some very serious messing around. He…he satisfied me, if you will."

"Oh, this is all my fault," Sarah said, her words filled with regret.

"*Now* you've decided to take the blame?" Libby accused. "I think you're a little late."

"I was the one who encouraged you to take more risks. I shouldn't have told you that. It can only lead to heartache."

"It doesn't have to," Libby said, trying to appear indifferent to the entire situation. "What happened between us was just one night. It doesn't have to happen again. I won't let it."

Sarah steered the car back into traffic and headed to Libby's house, her expression pensive. When she pulled to a stop on Charles Street, Sarah switched off the ignition and then turned to her. "Do you want it to happen again?"

"No!" Libby grabbed her things, shoved open the car door and hurried up the sidewalk, Sarah following close on her heels. "Yes!" She groaned. "I don't know what I want," she said, stomping up the front steps. "I just don't want to get hurt again." She grabbed the mail from the mailbox, then unlocked the front door and stepped inside.

Sarah followed her in. Libby kicked off her shoes, flopped down on the sofa and then distractedly began to sort the mail, searching for anything to take her mind off the chaos that Trey had created in her life. She picked out a plain envelope that was stuck between two catalogs, turning it over in her hands.

"What is it?" Sarah asked.

Libby shrugged and handed the envelope to her friend. "It's probably from the Throckmortons. They stopped by this morning to offer their sympathies. They're concerned about riffraff moving into the neighborhood. Their grandmother was a Parrish, you know, and they've never trusted the Marburys. Go ahead, read it."

Sarah opened the envelope and took out a single sheet of stationery. "I haven't stopped thinking about you since last night," she began. "With everything I touch, I feel your skin beneath my fingertips. With—"

Libby snatched the letter from Sarah's hand.

"I don't think that's from the Throckmortons,"

Sarah muttered, "unless they've decided to make a lifestyle change at age eighty."

Libby read the note silently, her heart slamming in her chest as her gaze skimmed over the tidy penmanship.

I haven't stopped thinking about you since last night. With everything I touch, I feel your skin beneath my fingertips. With every breeze that blows, I remember the warmth of your breath on my cheek. I taste your mouth, I smell your hair, I hear your soft cries for release. Every memory of that night is still fresh in my mind. And when I'm alone, I think about the next time and how it will be between us. You'll come to me, ready for more. And I'll wait, knowing that this time you'll please me. Why do I need you so much? Is this punishment for some long-ago sin or are we meant to take pleasure where we can find it? I'm here, close by, and this time, I'll wait for you. Don't make me wait too long.

"It's from him," Libby murmured, handing the note back to Sarah.

Sarah sat down on the sofa beside Libby and finished reading. "Wow," she murmured. "I can't believe he wrote this to you. I mean, Trey probably knows exactly how to please a woman in bed, but this…" She took a shaky breath and fanned herself with the letter. "This is so…it could make a girl… why hasn't anyone ever written a note like this to me?"

"How am I supposed to resist him?" Libby moaned, her voice thick with tightly checked tears.

"I don't think you are. No woman could resist a letter like this. It's not possible."

They both sat on the sofa for a long time, each of them taking turns rereading the note. When a knock sounded on the back door, both Sarah and Libby jumped to their feet.

"That's probably him," Sarah said.

"He said I was supposed to come to him!" Libby cried.

"Maybe he got tired of waiting." Sarah fussed with Libby's hair. "Try not to look so terrified. And call me. I want to know everything. And make sure you put on some pretty underwear. Men love that lacy black stuff."

Libby nodded, giving her friend a wan smile as Sarah hurried out the front door. She stood frozen in place, unsure of what to do next. If she ran upstairs to change her underwear, he might grow impatient and leave. And if she answered the door, then this would start all over again, this undeniable heat between the two of them. Did she really want to complicate her life like this? Even Trey wasn't aware of the power he held over her, the power to make her lose all sense of who she was and how she should behave.

Another knock echoed through the house and she cursed softly, then hurried to the kitchen. If she didn't put an end to this now, there was no telling what might happen. "He probably thinks I'm just some lonely, small-town spinster, happy to find a man— any man—willing to hop in my bed! And he wanders into town with his sexy smile and killer body, figuring he'll show me a good time before he wanders back out again."

By the time she reached the door, her indecision had been replaced by righteous resolution. She grabbed the door and swung it open, ready to send him packing. But as soon as she did, all the anger seemed to rush from inside her, like air from a pricked balloon.

He smiled, his blue eyes lighting up when he saw her. "Hey there," Trey said.

Libby held on to the door for balance as she shifted back and forth on her feet. "Hello." The word caught in her throat and she swallowed hard.

"I just thought I'd bring back your basket." He held it up. "I wanted to thank you again for the biscuits."

Libby opened the door a crack, grabbed the basket and then closed it. She knew the door was the only thing keeping her from falling into Trey's arms. "Thanks."

They stared at each other for a long moment and he smiled again. "I was wondering if you might want to go down to the river for a swim."

"The river?"

"Yeah. I know about the inlet. I used to swim there with my buddies. Your father chased us off a couple of times, but we'd always sneak back." He held up a coil of rope. "I thought we could string this up and make a swing."

"You want to go swimming?"

"Sure," Trey said. "Don't you?"

Frolicking around in the water with a barely dressed Trey would tempt any woman. He just looked so good without a shirt. Add wet hair and a little kissing and Libby would be lost. She swallowed hard. "I—I can't. I have a lot of work to do and I— well, I just can't. But thank you very much for asking. And—and feel free to go on your own."

Silence fell between them and Libby tried to think of a way to make a graceful exit. But when Trey pulled the screen door open, she realized that she'd missed her chance. She backed up as he stepped inside, retreating to the kitchen doorway.

"Libby, what's wrong?"

She forced a smile. "Nothing. I'm just not in the mood for a swim right now."

"What are you in the mood for? Because the way you're looking at me, I'm thinking you're probably in the mood for an argument. Am I wrong?"

"I don't want to argue with you, Trey." She tried to keep her tone light, but her voice cracked when he grabbed her around the waist and pulled her against his body.

Trey cupped her cheek in his hand, his gaze fixed on her mouth. "I don't want to argue either," he murmured.

He leaned forward and brushed a kiss across her lips and Libby felt her limbs go limp. How was she supposed to resist this? Every ounce of her being craved his touch, ached for the feel of his mouth on her body and longed for the release that she'd experienced with him.

"You don't regret what we did last night, do you?"

Mustering all her resolve, Libby pulled back. "No. I wish I did, but I don't. It was wonderful."

He frowned as he looked down at her. Could he see what it had cost her to admit the power he held over her? Did he know how close she was to complete and total surrender?

His hand slipped down from her face to her neck and then dropped lower, to her breast. He gently teased at her nipple through the silk blouse she wore. "I've been thinking about touching you all day long," he murmured with a teasing grin.

She thought back to that night twelve years ago, to the trust he'd broken. He'd promised to come back, promised that what they'd shared meant something to him. If she let him touch her again, then she'd be doomed to suffer that humiliation all over again.

Libby closed her eyes and tipped back her head; his hands sent frissons of desire through her body. She mustered the last shred of her resistance. "Please don't do this to me," she begged.

Her words stopped him short and he gasped softly, his hands dropping to his side. "What is this, Libby? Just because you deny the desire between us, it isn't going to go away."

She opened her eyes and found him staring down at her, his jaw tight, his eyes cold. A shiver raced through her. She didn't want it to go away. It was like an insidious, addictive drug—something she craved in spite of the danger.

"I'm willing to admit what I want. I want you, Libby, more than I've ever wanted any other woman in my life." He cursed softly, then took her face between his hands and kissed her. His tongue teased at her lips, gently forcing her to respond.

Against all her instincts, Libby opened beneath the assault, her arms slipping around his neck, her body pressing against the lean length of his. A knot of desire twisted inside of her, consuming her with need. She wanted his hands on her again, stripping away her clothes, parting her legs, making her moist and ready. It would take so little just to give up, to let him make love to her.

"Tell me I can't make you want me," he murmured against her mouth. "Tell me you don't do the same for me. I was there in your bed, Libby. I know what I made you feel."

She drew a ragged breath and backed out of his embrace, trying to keep her knees from buckling beneath her. "That was lust," Libby said, her voice thin and tight. "And a little bit of curiosity. But one night was enough."

His jaw twitched as he stared into her eyes, as if searching her soul for answers she didn't have. Libby prayed that he'd leave, that she wouldn't be faced with making a choice.

"One night every twelve years? Hell, if that's all I can hope for, then I guess I'll see you in another twelve." He turned and walked out, letting the door slam behind him.

Libby listened to his footsteps on the veranda and then on the stairs leading to the backyard. And when she was sure that he was gone for good, Libby slowly sank to the floor and buried her face in her knees.

Her life had been so simple until Trey had moved back to Belfort. And she'd cursed that simplicity, longed for someone or something to make her life exciting again. "Be careful what you wish for," she murmured, rubbing at knots of tension in her neck.

Never in a thousand years would she have wished for Trey's return. He'd touched her and she'd become seventeen again, filled with hopes and dreams, doubts and insecurities, and silly notions of romance.

She'd become infatuated with him all over again and there was nothing she could do to stop it.

Libby tipped her head back and sighed, fighting the tears that pressed at the corners of her eyes. Or maybe she'd just never stopped wanting him in the first place. Whatever it was about Trey, it didn't make any difference. If she didn't stop this irrational behavior, she'd be picking up the pieces of her heart for the rest of her life.

4

TREY SWUNG the Jeep onto Center Street and then took a sip of coffee from the mug he'd brought from home. The caffeine slowly pumped through his bloodstream, giving him a badly needed boost after another sleepless night.

For the past week, he'd spent the end of each day and the beginning of the next working on the house, conveniently avoiding the prospect of sleep. It made no sense at all, since it was impossible to sleep in the heat of the day. But he'd slipped into a routine of short catnaps whenever exhaustion overwhelmed him. Only then could he lie down without lapsing into fantasies about Libby Parrish.

He was due to travel to Savannah the next day to settle the sale of one of his father's properties. Perhaps an air-conditioned hotel room and sixty miles of space between him and Libby would result in a decent night's sleep.

Five long days and as many restless nights had passed since he'd made the mistake of returning her biscuit basket. At first, Trey had assumed he'd caught her at a bad time, maybe in the midst of a professional crisis. Then, he decided it might have been the heat. But since then, Libby had steadfastly avoided him and he'd been forced to draw the obvious conclusion—she wanted nothing more to do with him.

Trey wasn't quite sure how to take that. He'd never been a guy to doubt his abilities in the bedroom or to misread a woman's reaction to those abilities. Libby had enjoyed everything he'd done to her and he'd been certain it would lead to something more.

But now, he was faced with the realization that he'd made a mistake taking her letter seriously. She'd promised to write to him after that night they'd spent together twelve years ago and he'd never received a single piece of mail from her. Though Trey had written to her, after six letters, he'd been forced to admit that she wanted nothing more to do with him.

Why start it all up again, only to stop when things began to get interesting? Was she playing some sort of game with him? Trey shook his head. She'd accused him of playing games with her. What the hell was that letter all about if it wasn't about seduction? "Geez, I thought I understood women," he muttered. "But I don't know what the hell Libby Parrish is thinking."

He pulled the Jeep up in front of the drugstore. After he turned off the ignition, he rested his hands on the steering wheel and allowed his mind to fill with images of Libby. He'd never wanted a woman as much as he'd wanted her that night—and every night since then.

It had taken every bit of his willpower not to take their encounter to its logical resolution. When he'd begun, he'd assumed it had all been just a little fun between consenting adults. But somewhere after the first kiss and before her orgasm, his feelings had changed. And he had realized he wanted more than just sex. He wanted that connection back, that special something that they'd experienced as teenagers.

But what was that connection? It couldn't have been love, not at that age and not after just one night together. It had been much deeper than lust, though. He'd experienced only lust since then, and he knew exactly how it felt to want a woman's body but not her soul. What he'd shared with Libby, both in the past and in the present, had fallen into some strange gray area—more than lust, but not quite love.

Whatever it was, it didn't erase the fact that he still wanted her. He wanted to touch her at will, to slowly undress her and enjoy the beauty of her naked body. He wanted to draw her close and make her shudder with need. And more than anything, he wanted to possess her, to move inside of her until his control shattered and his desire was spent.

Trey could lose himself in the storm of sensations Libby made him feel. He could forget there were reasons why it would never work between them. In a few months, he'd be back in Chicago and Libby would be living her life as if he'd never touched her or kissed her or made her cry out in pleasure. Somehow, Trey was certain he'd feel the loss much more acutely than she would.

"So then stop thinking about her," he muttered as he jumped out of the Jeep. He looked both ways before jogging across the street to the drugstore. As he stepped inside the cool interior, Trey noticed a group of ladies at the cosmetics counter. They stopped their conversation to stare at him and then lowered their voices to a whisper.

He shrugged it off and headed down the center aisle in search of a bottle of aspirin. All the manual labor had taken a toll, leaving him with achy muscles and a nagging cramp in his neck. Maybe that's why he'd had trouble sleeping.

He caught sight of Harley Simpson at the far end of the aisle and waved at him. "I'm looking for the aspirin," Trey called.

Harley grabbed a bottle from the shelf as he passed and bustled up to Trey. "Here you are," he said. "That's the generic. No use payin' for the brand name."

"Thanks." Trey turned for the counter, but Harley reached out to stop him.

He bent closer to Trey and lowered his voice. "I want you to know that when it comes to the purchase of prophylactical items, you can count on Simpson's Drugstore to be discreet."

"Thank you," Trey said, taken aback by the man's comment. "I'll keep that in mind."

"Believe me, I understand how the gossips in this town work. You give them a little to chew on and they make a feast out of it."

"Are they talking about me?" Trey whispered.

"Well, I'm not one to go passin' it on, but you have been the subject of a fair amount of jawin' these last few days."

"Well, you can tell everyone if they have any questions, they can come directly to me. I'll tell them what they want to know."

"Are you sure you ought to be doin' that?" Harley asked. "The young lady in question might not want you sullyin' her reputation around town."

"The young lady?"

"Yeah. Libby Parrish. She's the one you've been keepin' company with. Now, I never believed all they said about her—that she was some ice queen or a cold fish. Still waters do tend to run deep, if you know what I mean. You look at Mrs. Simpson and she don't look it, but she's a regular hellcat in the bedroom and I—"

"People are talking about me and Libby Parrish?" Trey interrupted.

"Well, yeah. Story is you spent the night with her last week."

Trey glanced around the store to find several of the patrons staring at him. So that's what this was all about. He'd noticed people acting strangely around him, suddenly going quiet, sending curious glances his way. But how the hell had they found out about him and Libby? He hadn't said a word to anyone.

Trey turned away from Harley and headed to the door. He tossed the aspirin on the counter as he passed, not bothering to buy it. Had Libby heard the gossip? Was that what was keeping her at a distance? He shoved open the door and then stepped out onto the sidewalk, the midday heat hitting him like a wet blanket.

As he jogged across the street to his Jeep, he saw Libby leave the post office. Trey changed direction and headed her off, joining her in front of Harrington's Hardware. "I have to talk to you," he said, catching hold of her elbow and steering her around the corner. He glanced both ways and then stepped into the shade of the side entrance to the hardware store.

"What are you doing?" Libby asked, pulling out of his grasp. "Do you want the whole town gossiping about us?"

His breath suddenly died in his throat. God, she was beautiful. In just a week, he'd forgotten how pale her hair was, how it fell so softly around her face and how it smelled like flowers when he got close to her. "I'm afraid they already are," Trey said.

Libby gasped, her green eyes growing wide. "What? Why?"

"They know we spent a night together."

"Who did you tell?"

"No one," Trey replied. "I figured you'd told someone." He reached up to tuck a strand of hair behind her ear, anxious to touch her again.

She avoided his gaze, choosing to stare at his chest. "No! No one…except—no, she'd never tell anyone. Sarah's my friend."

"It doesn't really matter," Trey said, frustrated that she refused to look him in the eye. "Besides, we're both adults. Our private lives are private. Let them talk."

"You don't have to live in this town," she snapped. "You're just passing through."

Trey pushed aside his growing anger, grabbing her chin and forcing her gaze up to his. "What kind of game are you playing here, Libby?"

"What are you talking about? You're the one playing games."

"I was there that night. You act like you don't remember what it was like between us. Can you stop thinking about it? Because I can't. I touched your body," he said, smoothing his palm over her bare shoulder. "I felt you come in my arms. That was real, whether you want to admit it or not."

"Stop it!" she hissed.

"I don't think you want me to stop. I think this little game excites you. I'm forbidden fruit, a Marbury, and as long as what we share has to be hidden, you enjoy it more." Trey backed her up against the door, bracing his hands on either side of her head. "Say it, Libby. Just say you don't want me and I'll go away. I promise."

She closed her eyes for a moment and then met his gaze defiantly. He considered kissing her, trying to prove his point with actions rather than words. Trey leaned closer, searching for some sign she'd respond. "Say it," he demanded, so close he felt her breath on his lips, craved the taste of her tongue.

"All right. I do want you. Are you happy now?"

Trey reached up and brushed his thumb across her lower lip. "Yeah, I'm happy."

She turned into his touch for a moment and then shook her head. One second she was there, waiting for him to kiss her; the next, she'd ducked down and slipped out of his grasp. "Now, keep your promise and leave me alone!" Libby shouted as she hurried down the street.

Trey started after her and then thought better of it. "This isn't over, Libby. We're not done yet," he called.

When he turned back around, he saw a small crowd gathered at the door of the hardware store, peering at him through the glass. "All right, the show's over," he yelled. "Nothing more to see here."

Cursing softly, Trey started down the street to his Jeep. No wonder he'd left this damn town far behind him. He couldn't sneeze in Belfort without half the town speculating about the state of his health. Now they had something much juicier to contemplate—a steamy sexual relationship between a Parrish and Marbury.

"Let them talk," Trey muttered. "And as long as they are, I'm going to try like hell to give them something new to talk about."

He wasn't done with Libby, not by a long shot. There was something between them and he wasn't leaving town until he found out exactly what it was.

"My mother is going to kill me," Libby murmured.

Sarah sighed. "You know what they say. If it's not one thing, it's your mother."

"And after she kills me, she's going to kill herself," Libby muttered. "Trey's father made my father's life miserable. They were constantly in competition, and I'm sure the stress of it took its toll. If Daddy hears that Trey is back in town, he might just move back to Belfort and start this whole feud up again."

"I think you're making an awful lot of a few rumors," Sarah commented as she picked at her chicken salad. She stabbed a grape and popped it in her mouth. "People are talking. So far, it's just speculation. Besides, I think your reputation could do with a little tarnishing."

"I'm not worried about my reputation," Libby said. "I'm sick to death of people thinking I'm something I'm not. I have needs just like any other woman." She frowned and then sat down at the kitchen table. "I just wish I knew where the rumor got started."

The front doorbell rang and Sarah glanced up at Libby. "Maybe that's Trey, ready to make some new rumors."

"I don't think so. I'm pretty sure he's going to be

staying away from me after our little encounter yesterday morning."

Libby pushed up from the table and walked through the wide entrance hall that spanned the depth of the house. Sarah joined her a few seconds later to find Carlisle Whitby standing on the other side of the screen door. She frowned. Carlisle usually made his deliveries in the morning.

"Hello, Carlisle," Libby murmured. "What can I do for you?"

"I have your mail here, Lisbeth. I thought there might be something important."

"You can just leave the mail in the box," Libby suggested as gently as she could.

"I—I wonder if we might have a word," he said. Carlisle shot a glance over to Sarah. "In private."

Libby stifled a smile as she heard Sarah giggle behind her. She stepped out onto the veranda and followed Carlisle to the steps. "What is it?"

"I've been hearing rumors around town," he said, staring at his government-issue shoes. "Rumors that have called into question your reputation."

"Carlisle, I think that—"

"No, let me finish what I've come to say. I don't know the source of these scurrilous accusations, though I do have my suspicions." Carlisle paused to send a hostile look in the direction of Trey's house. "But I'm determined to find out and once I do, I plan to make sure that the scoundrel pays."

"Scoundrel?" Libby bit her bottom lip. "I'm not sure I've ever heard that word used in conversation, Carlisle. Have you been reading a little too much *Gone with the Wind* lately?"

"I understand. You're using humor to hide your distress. But I'm here to offer my assistance."

"Are you going to call this person out?" Libby teased. "Pistols at ten paces? I appreciate the gesture, Carlisle, but I can take care of this myself."

"I only wish that dueling was still legal. But, since it isn't, I'd like to offer my services in another way. I'd like to take you out on a date. It would help to face these rumors straight on, to show everyone in Belfort that they couldn't possibly be true. And to be seen in the company of an employee of the U.S. Postal Service might restore your reputation to its former unimpeachable status."

Libby cleared her throat and forced a smile. "I appreciate the offer, Carlisle, but I'm sure the rumors will die down over time. Besides, the scoundrel, as you call him, will be leaving town in a month or two and this will all be forgotten."

"It can't be too soon for me," Carlisle said. "I found illegal mail in his box the other day. You can't trust a man like that." He nodded and then started down the steps. "Oh, I forgot to give you this." He handed Libby a slip of paper. "There's a package waiting for you at the post office with postage due. I'd be happy to pay the postage and bring it over to you after my shift."

"No, I'll take care of this myself. It's just a cookbook I ordered. Thanks for your concern, Carlisle. You'd better get back to work. I wouldn't want to put you off schedule."

Carlisle hoisted his bag onto his shoulder and hurried off down the sidewalk, his stubby legs carrying him as fast as they could. Libby sighed and then walked back inside the house.

Sarah was waiting for her in the kitchen. "Good grief," she muttered. "I think all that school paste Carlisle ate as a kid has seriously affected his brain."

"He was concerned about all the rumors."

"Or maybe it's you that's affected his brain," Sarah teased. "Remember when he jumped off the top of the monkey bars just to impress you? Poor kid broke his leg."

"He just asked me out. He thought it might help to be seen in the company of a U.S. postal carrier." Libby slid into a chair at the table and cupped her chin in her hand. "You know what the really awful thing is? For a moment, I actually considered accepting."

"Carlisle Whitby?"

"He's not so bad. He's a little short and little bald and he still lives at home with his mama, but other than that, he's all right."

"And after all, you don't have any other prospects on the horizon."

"I'm serious," Libby said. "What has my life come to?"

"A choice," Sarah said. "Taking the safe route with Carlisle or—"

"Risking it all with a guy like Trey?" Libby finished. "I thought you weren't in favor of risk."

"Well, I've been thinking about it and I know he hurt you in the past, Lib, but you're a grown-up now. If you don't figure out how you feel about him, you may never be able to move on with your life. You can control this—you can decide where it goes and when it stops. And maybe, if you dump him this time, you can balance the scales a bit."

"I suppose I could," Libby murmured. "But don't

you think that's like playing with fire? When I'm with Trey, I just forget all common sense."

"Then take control," Sarah said. "Make him want you on your terms. And if he can't handle that, then walk away."

"My terms," Libby said.

Sarah picked up her plate and took it to the sink, then wiped her hands on a dish towel. "I've got a meeting at the station tomorrow to go over the Web site design for the new season. Do you want to drive in with me and see what they have planned?"

Libby shook her head. "No, right now, I don't want to think about work. I just want to relax and think about my...options."

"Don't forget, you've got that trip to New Orleans next weekend. They've set you up in a very nice hotel and you'll be doing a book signing and a radio interview along with your seminar. I've got your itinerary all set."

"I'll look at it later." Libby grabbed a magazine from the table and slowly fanned herself. "I hear it's supposed to rain tonight. Maybe I'll finally be able to sleep."

Sarah waved as she walked out of the kitchen, leaving Libby alone with her thoughts. She'd seduced Trey once when she was seventeen. She should be able to do much better now that she was a little older.

Libby pushed back from the table and retrieved the letter from the drawer beneath the phone. She'd contemplated burning it, so that she'd never have to look at it again. But she'd nearly memorized it, along with all the feelings that the words evoked.

Passion had never been a priority in her relationships in the past. After her first experience with Trey, she'd always measured her romances against that night, a night that, over time, had become mythic in her mind.

"Closure," Libby muttered, the concept coming to her at that very moment. Perhaps that was why she couldn't put her feelings about Trey in the past. There were so many questions and very few answers. Why hadn't he ever tried to contact her after that night? How did he feel about what they'd shared? Did he remember it in the same way she did?

Libby cursed softly. She was nearly thirty years old and she was still stuck reliving an event that had happened when she was a teenager. This wasn't just about closure; it was about her inability to move her life forward!

The patterns of her life had been set early. When she was younger, she had preferred to stay at home or study at the library, rather than participate in school activities. After she'd graduated from high school, she'd chosen the same small liberal arts college in Savannah that Sarah was attending and continued to live at home. And when she couldn't find a job with her art history degree, her mother had suggested they work on a cookbook. Even the television show had been Sarah's idea, instigated after she took a job with the PBS station in Charleston.

Libby had always waited for life to happen to her, waited for that one big event that would send her future in a new and exciting direction. Now she had a chance to *make* things happen; whether they turned out good or bad in the end, at least she wouldn't be sitting around waiting.

With a sigh, she glanced down at the letter. Yes, she'd seduced him once. But he wasn't the same high school boy who'd made love to her all those years ago. Seducing a man experienced in the sexual arts was a whole different matter. She'd have to give him something totally unexpected, something he'd never be able to forget.

And when I'm alone, I think about the next time and how it will be between us. You'll come to me, ready for more. And I'll wait, knowing that you'll please me.

Her mind wandered back to the night he'd appeared in her garden, standing in the moonlight and waiting for her to ask him in. They hadn't bothered with words then; instead, they let the heat of their passion determine the course of events.

A tremor raced through her body at the thought of what they had shared, the thought of giving Trey the same kind of pleasure that he'd given her. Libby refolded the letter and tucked it back inside the drawer.

She'd have to make her move soon. The longer she waited, the more reasons she'd find to back out. But she needed an opening line, some way to indicate her feelings had changed since the last time they'd seen each other. With a tiny smile, Libby yanked open the freezer door and pulled out a pineapple upside-down cake that she'd made a few days ago.

She'd intended to give it to Trey anyway, so why not use it now? She took the pan and popped it in the oven, then turned the heat to low. If it were warm, he'd think she'd just baked it, and maybe he'd invite her in to share a piece with him. Who knows where a little cake and conversation might lead?

While the cake was warming, Libby raced upstairs and rummaged through her clothes for a fresh cotton sundress and her sexiest underwear. Taking a shower might wash away her courage, so she splashed water on her face and ran a damp cloth over her sticky skin. Then she applied a dab of mascara and a bit of lipstick and headed back to the kitchen.

She flipped the cake onto a plate, decorated it with a few rosettes from a can of whipped cream, then headed out the back door. Drawing a deep breath and marshaling her resolve, Libby walked around the azalea bushes into Trey's backyard. It was nearly dinnertime, so he'd probably be hungry. She could offer to make him something to eat before she actually got down to the business of seduction. "After all, I'm probably better at cooking and baking than making a man crazy with desire," Libby muttered.

The back door to Trey's house was propped open and Libby stepped inside the kitchen. Unlike her home, the old Sawyer place was in a sad state. The kitchen dated back to the 1920s and everything in it was covered with a thin coating of dust. An ancient stove and icebox were the only conveniences.

"Hello!" she called.

A few seconds later, Beau ran into the room, his black nose covered with white plaster dust. He wriggled around her legs, his tail thumping on the floor. "Sorry, no biscuits today."

Beau's entrance was quickly followed by Trey's. He stopped short as he entered the kitchen. "Hi," he said.

He was dressed in his usual attire of baggy shorts and sport sandals, but this time, he was bare-chested, his skin coated with the same layer of plaster dust that coated everything else in the house. Libby's breath caught in her throat as she let her gaze drift along his body, over his wide, muscular chest to his rippled abdomen. His arms and legs were long and well muscled, and his strong hands rested on impossibly narrow hips.

She swallowed hard, her eyes watering slightly from all the dust in the house. She could feel her pulse racing and her mouth had gone dry, making it difficult to speak. Had she been bolder, she might have been able to walk directly into his arms and kiss him, but Libby couldn't be sure how he'd react.

She didn't want to deal with the preliminaries, the nervous moments and the stilted conversation. Libby wanted to begin where they'd left off the night of the storm—hot, eager, uninhibited. "I thought it was about time I brought that cake you requested."

He glanced over his shoulder, the tension evident in the set of his jaw. "And I thought you didn't want anything more to do with me. Now you bring me a cake? Kind of mixed signals, don't you think, Lib?"

"I'm sorry about yesterday. I shouldn't have taken my frustrations out on you. I know you didn't say anything."

"I've never been one to kiss and tell."

Libby smiled ruefully, wondering how she might convince him to touch her again. She glanced down at his fingers and a shiver ran through her at the memory of what he'd done to her that night in her bed. "That's a very good policy, especially in Belfort."

They stood in silence for a long moment; then Libby held out the cake. "I think you'll enjoy it. It's a really good recipe. It's from an old electric company cookbook." Damn the cake! Right now, she was ready to toss it over her shoulder and throw herself into his arms. Conversing about cake was not a good start to a seduction. "Don't you want it?" she asked.

"I think you know what I want," Trey said, his gaze never wavering.

She swallowed hard. If she was waiting for an opening, then this was it. He'd spelled it out in the letter so she could have no doubts. Libby turned around and set the cake on the counter. "I do know what you want," she murmured.

But when she turned back to him, he was staring down at a blueprint spread over the kitchen table. "Listen, I'd really like to chat, but I've got a lot of work to do. I've got the plaster guys tearing up the dining room and the plumber is working on the bathroom upstairs. You probably should get out of here before they wander in or we'll be subject to a whole new round of rumor and innuendo."

Libby felt anger flare inside of her. So this was the way it would be. A battle for control. Though he seemed so cool and distant, when Libby met his gaze, she saw the truth. He wanted her as much as she wanted him. His eyes couldn't lie.

His gaze dropped to her lips and she knew he was thinking about kissing her. Libby slowly drew her tongue along her lower lip, inviting him to give in to the urge. "We wouldn't want that," she murmured.

He frowned. Then, with a soft curse, he snatched up the blueprint. "You'd better go." With that, Trey turned and walked out of the room, leaving Libby to wonder whether she had any chance at all of controlling Trey. As long as they were using sex as a weapon, one of them was bound to lose. She just didn't want it to be her.

"Cake, bad idea," she muttered as she walked out of the house. "Timing, also very bad. And I could probably sex up the outfit a little bit."

This whole seduction was going to take much more thought and planning. Libby frowned. Trey had accomplished his objective with so much ease. Why was it so difficult for her?

"LOOKS LIKE THE electrician did a good job," Wiley Boone said. "I can sign off on that, but you need to call the plumber back and have him put a new shut-off valve on the main line. You can't count on those old valves on the meter anymore."

"I've got the heating and air-conditioning guy coming in next week, so I'll need you back to inspect that job."

"You sure you want to spend all that money on a house you're just gonna turn around and sell? Wasn't that your plan?"

Trey leaned back against the kitchen counter, crossing his arms over his chest. That was the question he'd been asking himself. What was his plan, not just for this house, but for Libby? After all her protests, she'd appeared at his door, cake in hand, ready to be friends again.

But he'd seen right through her platonic facade. She wanted him to kiss her again, to pull her into his arms and run his hands over her body. This dance they were doing with each other was designed to drive him mad and unless she capitulated completely, he wasn't going to give in.

"I 'spose it'll increase the value of the house," Wiley continued.

"And it will make my stay here a lot more comfortable," Trey added.

The building inspector nodded. "Yep, it does get a little warm 'round these parts." Wiley's eyes fixed on a spot next to Trey. "That looks like a mighty fine cake you got there. Pineapple upside-down is just about my most favorite. Is that one of Libby Parrish's cakes? 'Cause I heard that you and her were on cake bakin' terms."

Was this a new Belfort euphemism for sex, Trey wondered? "I'd really like to know where that rumor got started."

"No tellin'," Wiley said, still eyeing the cake. "You plannin' to eat that cake, 'cause if you let it sit there, it's just gonna dry up."

"Would you like a piece?" Trey asked.

"Don't mind if I do," Wiley said.

Trey rummaged around for a knife, cut a generous slice of the cake and put it on a paper plate for the inspector. "So you'll come back late next week?"

"That Libby Parrish sure makes a good cake. I tell ya, she's gonna make some man a fine wife. And I don't have to say, I'd sure like to be that man."

"Have you and Libby dated?" Trey asked.

"No. But I'm thinkin' on askin' her out. You think she'd go out with me?"

Trey wasn't sure what to say. He certainly was in no position to encourage Wiley, but he was also fairly sure that Libby wouldn't accept. He just shrugged, walked Wiley to the front door and shook his hand before he left. Wandering back through the house, he took stock of the work he'd accomplished so far.

The cracked plaster had been repaired, the ornate carved moldings had been restored and layers of paint had been scraped off the old mantels in the dining room and front parlor. He had to paint the walls and strip the pine floors, but after that, he could move on to the upstairs. Central heat and air would make the house as comfortable as it was beautiful.

He ran his fingers through his dusty hair, then shook his head. Right now, he needed a long swim in a cool river. Trey grabbed a beer from the refrigerator and headed out the back door, unbuttoning his shirt as he walked. But he stopped in his tracks the moment he saw Libby standing on the veranda, Beau sitting at her feet.

"Your dog's been in my rose garden again."

Trey shouldn't have been surprised to see her, but it was her appearance that took his breath away. She wore a clingy black dress, barely more than a slip, made of a fabric that seemed to mould to her body. The hem was high and the neckline low, showing off more skin that Libby normally displayed. And her blond hair, usually pulled back in a haphazard knot was a riot of loose waves that brushed her bare shoulders.

Trey opened his mouth to warn her off. He wasn't going to get sucked into this game she was playing. But Libby shook her head and pressed her finger to her lips. "Don't speak," she murmured. "If you say anything, I'll walk away."

His gaze fixed on her as she approached and he felt his heart start to pound. She carried a silk scarf that brushed along her leg as she walked, and his fingers twitched as Trey imagined drawing the dress up and over her head and revealing the naked body beneath.

When she reached the top of the steps, she slowly sauntered over to him, her hips swaying suggestively as she walked. "I warned you about the dog, didn't I?"

Trey groaned inwardly, heat already pumping through his veins. She wasn't here to scold him about Beau, or to pay another social call. From the look in Libby's eyes, she had other things on her mind.

"I've been trying to figure you out, Trey Marbury," Libby murmured, walking around him, letting her body brush up against his as she did. "I'm wondering why you came back to town and decided to buy this house. And why you were so determined to seduce me. And, most especially, why you wrote me that letter."

Trey frowned. He wasn't sure what letter she was referring to—maybe one of the six he sent all those years ago—but he didn't feel the urge to question her at the present time. Besides, talking was against the rules and now that Trey had decided to get back in the game, he didn't want to break them.

She flipped the scarf over his shoulder and then drew the fabric forward along his neck, the feel of it like a caress. "But then, I realized it doesn't really matter. You said it the other day. We're both adults. We should be able to handle a purely physical attraction." This time as she circled him, she let her hand brush up against his backside. And when she came around again, her fingers drifted over his crotch, lingering there for a few seconds before moving on.

Trey bit back a moan. If she was bent on torturing him, then she'd made a good start. He felt himself growing hard, his erection pressing against the fabric of his shorts. Though he ought to have been embarrassed by his immediate reaction, somehow, he knew Libby's actions were having the effect she desired. She hadn't come here to talk; she'd come to entice him.

"I've decided I might have overreacted earlier. I'll admit, I haven't been able to stop thinking about that night you came to my room. And given our mutual desires, I think we can both get what we want," she continued. She looked up at him, her green eyes wide. "Don't you agree?"

Trey nodded.

This time as she circled him, she dragged the scarf across his feet. She caught one of his hands as she passed, then looped the silk around his wrist. Trey laughed softly as she took his other arm and knotted his hands together behind him.

"I suppose you're wondering what I'm doing." She gently pushed him back against the railing of the veranda and then tied the loose ends of the scarf to the balustrade. "I think we should make this all about your pleasure tonight. That's what you want, isn't it?"

He couldn't think of an objection, so Trey shrugged. Sure, he'd take his pleasure, or come close. But he'd find a way to free his hands and return the favor before things got too out of hand.

Glancing down, he watched her unbutton his shirt, so slowly that the simple act of undressing him turned undeniably erotic. When Libby was finished, she pushed the shirt off his shoulders and shoved it down to his wrists, leaving his torso bare.

Her fingertips trailed over his skin, sending a current buzzing to his nerve ends. Trey tipped his head back and closed his eyes, focusing on the sensation of her hands on his body. The lazy pace of her caress piqued his desire and he found himself wanting more. But it was clear Libby wasn't going to race through this. She was going to take her time in seducing him, and he anticipated a fight to maintain control.

When her lips pressed against his skin, Trey opened his eyes again and looked down at her. He drew a deep breath, inhaling the scent of her hair, the strands brushing at his chin. He longed to taste her lips, to steal a kiss. But Libby's tongue delved lower, circling around his nipple, teasing it to a peak.

A low groan slipped from Trey's lips followed by a soft chuckle. Again, he was stunned by the sudden shift in her mood. She'd gone from insecure to wanton in a matter of hours, and he found himself captivated by the contrast.

Why had no man managed to capture her heart? Libby was sweet and sexy and smart, everything a man could want from a lover. For now, she had chosen to turn her affections toward him, and he wasn't about to question his good fortune.

As she kissed his chest, Libby's palms smoothed over his belly, her fingers dipping provocatively beneath his waistband. Then suddenly, her fingers were at the front of his shorts cupping him, the fabric providing a flimsy barrier to her touch.

"You're driving me crazy," he murmured.

"You're not supposed to speak."

"If you kiss me, I'll stop," Trey bargained. "I promise."

She looked up and smiled at him, the beauty of her face sending another wave of heat through his body. Libby slowly worked her way back across familiar territory and then covered his lips with hers, her tongue tantalizing, taking possession of his mouth. She'd become the aggressor and Trey found the new dynamic between them very stimulating.

Trey's mind spun as he lost himself in the kiss. How the hell was he supposed to last? He was lucky his hands were tied behind his back, because just the thought of touching her was bringing him right to the edge.

"Is this it?" she murmured, her lips trailing down his chest again. "Is this your fantasy?"

"This is better than any fantasy I ever had," Trey replied.

As her fingers dropped to the waistband of his shorts, Trey sucked in a sharp breath. He'd never been seduced like this before, never allowed a woman such absolute control over his desire. But Libby had taken it and he was happy to step back and see where this led.

A moment later, his shorts slid over his hips, and then she tugged on his boxers. His shaft caught in the waistband, then sprung free, completely erect and achingly sensitive. He didn't have time to contemplate what came next. When her lips closed over him, Trey lost the ability to think at all.

Slowly, she began to move, taking him in before drawing away, sending wild currents coursing through his body. He had to close his eyes because watching her was too much. She brought him close several times, but Trey yanked himself back from the edge, wanting to enjoy her just a moment longer, knowing that to come would mean an end to this sweet torture.

Her tongue teased, running from the base of his shaft, then lingering on the tip. Trey's heart slammed in his chest and his breathing came in short gasps. He murmured her name, but it wasn't enough. Trey needed his hands free, to run his fingers through her hair, to slow her pace so that it wouldn't be over too quickly. But instead, he was forced to concentrate on a single point of contact between them.

And then her fingers took over and she worked her way back up his chest. He caught her lips with his and kissed her, drinking in the taste like a man parched with thirst. As her body pressed against his and her stroke quickened, Trey plunged his tongue into her mouth, imagining what it would be like to move inside her.

A moment later, he exploded in her hand. The orgasm sent waves of pleasure washing over him. She slowed her caress, nuzzling into his neck as she took him to the very limits of his pleasure. Trey shuddered and then groaned, sensitive in the aftermath of his orgasm.

"What do you want now? Tell me," Libby murmured, smoothing her hand over his damp belly.

"I want to make love to you," he whispered in her ear. He bit back another groan. "But I don't think I can."

Libby stepped back and looked into his face. "Why not? Did I wear you out?"

A grin twitched at the corners of his mouth. "I'm

probably good to go another time or two," he said. "I just don't have any protection."

"What about the—"

"I didn't buy them. If I buy condoms here in town, everyone is going to know what you and I are up to. I figure I'm going to have to go to Charleston or Savannah to avoid the gossips."

"Then I think you'd better take a road trip," Libby suggested. "And call me when you get back." She slowly drew away, then gave him a quick kiss before sauntering to the steps. "I'll be seein' you, Trey Marbury."

"Wait a second," Trey called. "There are a lot of other things we could do that wouldn't require condoms."

"No, I think it's best to wait," she said. "We might just get carried away and…well, we'll save that for later." She gave him a little wave.

"You're just going to leave me tied up here?"

"Now we're even," she said, laughing softly.

"If you untie me, I'll invite you in for cake. I have this really great cake."

"No, I don't think so," Libby said.

Trey didn't want to her to leave. He scrambled for something, anything to keep her just a few minutes longer. "I'm going to Savannah tomorrow on business. Why don't you come with me?" Trey offered.

"I think you can pick up condoms on your own."

"We can get out of town and spend some time together, without all the gossips wondering what we're up to. We'll have lunch, take a carriage ride or maybe a walk along the harbor."

"I can't," Libby said in a teasing voice.

"You can't or you won't?"

"Does it matter?"

"We're going to have to talk about this thing between us sooner or later, Libby. It's not going to go away."

"Oh, it will go away," she murmured.

"How? When?"

"When you leave town." With that she turned on her heel and hurried across the lawn. A few seconds later, she disappeared behind the azalea bushes.

Trey closed his eyes and tipped his head back, drawing in a deep breath of the humid night air. This whole thing felt like a dream, like some heat-induced hallucination meant to drive him crazy.

It took him a few minutes to untie the knots and when he did, Trey reached down and adjusted the front of his boxers, shaking his head. He'd known a lot of women in his life, but he'd never met a woman as mercurial and mysterious as Lisbeth Parrish. He could never predict where he stood with her day to day. One moment, she was yelling at him, the next, she was running away, and the next, she was seducing him.

Trey held the scarf up to his nose, the scent of her perfume wafting off of the silk. He smiled as he walked back inside. He had a life waiting for him back in Chicago, but suddenly he'd grown very fond of Belfort. There were things in this town a man might not be able to find anywhere else in the world—a decent bowl of grits, a beautiful old house filled with great architectural details and, of course, a woman who could arouse him with a simple smile.

5

"YOU'RE GOING OUT with who?"

"Whom. And you heard me," Libby said. "I have a date with Carlisle Whitby. I called him up this morning and accepted his offer. We're having dinner at Tarrington's tonight. He's picking me up at five."

"I can't believe this," Sarah said, raking her hand through her auburn hair. "You're throwing over a guy like Trey Marbury for a dweeb like Carlisle. The man collects Civil War bullets. Little bitty pieces of lead that he finds with his metal detector. He spends his weekends running around dressed like a Confederate general. If you date him, then you might as well give up any hope of a normal guy ever asking you out."

"There are no normal guys in Belfort." Libby rose out of the wicker chair that overlooked her garden and grabbed her empty glass. "Don't you see? It's the perfect plan," she explained. "If I date Carlisle, it will deflect all the gossip. And that's all I really want to do."

She grabbed the pitcher from the small table near the back door, refilled her glass and then held the pitcher out to Sarah. Her friend shook her head. "Why are you so worried about the gossip?" she asked.

"I might as well tell you I have decided to engage

in a purely sexual relationship with Trey. And I don't want everyone in town to speculate about the details. Otherwise, I'm going to be stuck explaining what happened between us after he leaves. For the next five years, everyone is going to feel sorry for me, how poor Libby Parrish got taken in by that scoundrel, Trey Marbury. But if I can deflect some of the attention to Carlisle, then all the better for me and Trey, don't you think?"

"You know what I think? I think the heat has finally fried your brain." Sarah dipped a paper napkin in her iced tea and tried to dab at Libby's forehead, but Libby slapped away her hand. "How do you think Carlisle is going to feel when he finds out you used him? Sleeping with one guy while you're dating another is not a very nice thing to do."

Libby stared at her fingernails, studying her manicure while she came up with a decent reply. "Maybe it's not the nicest thing in the world to do. But don't you think Carlisle might get a little out of it, too?"

"What? Are you going to put out for him? Are you and Carlisle going to drive down to Walker's Point and smooch in the back of his mama's station wagon?"

"I was referring to the fact that dating me might make Carlisle look a little better in the eyes of some of the other single women in Belfort."

Sarah frowned. "Well, I suppose that might happen. I hear he's been chasing after Jenny Dalton. She's a checker down at the Winn-Dixie."

"It's only going to be a few dates. Just until everyone stops talking about Trey and me. And Carlisle is the one who volunteered to help restore my reputation, so I shouldn't have to feel guilty."

"Lib, are you sure you have this thing under control? Because it doesn't sound like you really know what you're doing. I know what a romantic you are. How can you be so nonchalant about this?"

"Because I know Trey is leaving. And I know he's not the kind of man who'd want to stay here in Belfort and marry me and raise a bunch of children. So it's simple. For once, I'm going to be practical and take this relationship for exactly what it is—an exciting, exhilarating sexual carnival ride that will come to an end."

Sarah turned her empty glass around and around in her hands as she pondered Libby's revelation. "Somehow, I don't think it's as simple as you make it sound."

Libby reached over and grabbed her best friend's hand. "You don't have to worry."

"I'm never going to stop worrying about you, Lib. We've been friends for far too long." She pushed out of her chair and set her glass down on the table. "I have to go. My folks invited me over for dinner tonight and I'm supposed to bring the dessert. You don't have a spare pie or cake in your refrigerator, do you?"

"There's a bourbon pecan pie in the freezer. Throw it in the oven when you serve dinner and it should be nice and warm when you're finished."

"Thanks," she said. "I'll see you later. And behave tonight. The last thing I want is to have to squelch rumors about you and Carlisle Whitby. Don't let him seduce you with all that mailman talk."

Libby giggled. "I won't." She sighed softly as she sat back and sipped at her iced tea, staring out at the garden, lush and green. The scent of roses hung in the air and Libby closed her eyes and smiled. An image of Trey, naked and aroused, drifted through her mind and she let it linger there. There was no doubt in her mind that they'd be together again. Now that she'd made the decision, the rest seemed to be quite simple.

"Hey there."

Libby opened her eyes to find the subject of her fantasy standing on the back steps, as if she'd summoned him merely by will. He was dressed in a starched white shirt and trousers, his tie undone and his usually mussed hair combed neatly. "You're back," she said.

"I am." He slowly climbed the steps. "I wanted to return this," Trey said, pulling her scarf out from behind his back.

Libby blushed as she took the scarf from his fingers. "I guess you managed to get free then."

"Yeah. Wiley Boone untied me this morning when he dropped off another building permit."

Libby's eyes went wide. "You spent the night—"

"No," Trey said. "But next time you decide to tie me up, it would be nice if you untied me afterward." He paused, sending her a devilish grin. "So, are you planning to tie me up again, Libby?"

She shrugged, pleased with the hint of challenge in his voice. "I'm not sure. Did you enjoy being tied up?"

"Oh, yeah," Trey said. "In fact, you can tie me up whenever you want, just as long as you make me feel like that again."

Libby's blush deepened, making her cheeks hot. "I'm glad you liked it."

Trey strolled up the steps and leaned against the railing in front of her, his long legs crossed and his hands braced beside him. There were times when Libby couldn't breathe for looking at him. He was by far the sexiest man she'd ever met. He had an easy charm about him, a way of making her feel as if she was the sexiest person in his world.

"You know, I was serious about getting out of town. Why don't we drive down to Savannah tonight? We could see a movie, go out to dinner and rent an expensive hotel room."

"You just came back from Savannah."

"Then we'll go to Charleston."

Though Libby was tempted to accept his offer, her plans with Carlisle were more important to the future of her relationship with Trey. "I can't. Not tonight."

He chuckled. "Why, do you have a date?"

Libby's smiled faded slightly. "I do have a date."

He nodded slowly, as if trying to hide his reaction behind a bland expression. "A date. Well, that's interesting. And just who would be taking you out tonight?"

"Carlisle Whitby."

Trey gasped and then laughed. "The mailman? You're going out with our mailman?"

"Yes. Are you jealous?"

Trey shrugged. "No. Hell, if Carlisle is your type, then I can't compete. He's got the mailbag and the uniform and that cute little truck with the steering wheel on the wrong side. I don't have a chance against a guy like that."

"He's not my type," Libby said. "And I'm only going out with him because I'm hoping it will put an end to all the talk around town about us. And it's just dinner at Tarrington's."

Trey grabbed her hands and pulled her to her feet. "Forget about all the talk. It's just speculation anyway." He bent his head and brushed a kiss across her lips. "Call Carlisle and tell him you have other plans. We'll get out of here and do something fun." He nuzzled her neck, nipping at it playfully. "I'll let you tie me up again. Or, if you want, I'll tie you up."

"No!" Libby said, pulling out of his embrace. She was supposed to be in control, not him! How easily he was able to take that control from her with just a little kiss or an innocent caress. He had to understand that there were limits to how far she was willing to go. "Not tonight."

He frowned, his gaze searching her expression for some clue to her reaction. "I thought we'd gotten past this. You want me, I want you. It's all pretty simple when you think about it."

"And that's the way I want to keep it," Libby said. "Simple. And very private."

"Fine," Trey said. "Great. The next time you want me, just write me another letter." With that, he turned and jogged down the steps.

Libby gasped. Another letter? Anger bubbled up inside of her. She'd done that twelve years ago and all it had brought her was regret. He'd stolen her heart back then and he was trying his damnedest to do it again. But she wasn't going to let him.

Maybe Sarah had been right. What seemed like a simple plan had suddenly turned complicated. If she knew what was good for her, she would learn to accept life as it was before Trey Marbury came back into town.

But now that she'd had a taste of excitement, it was awfully hard to go back.

TREY SLID onto a bar stool and ordered a whiskey neat from the bartender at Tarrington's. He glanced around at the other patrons, then thought about tossing some money on the bar and leaving. Getting caught up in this silly plan of Libby's was tantamount to admitting he had serious feelings for her. Here he was, ready to intrude on her date with another man, simply because the thought of sharing Libby with any other man—even Carlisle Whitby— was too much to bear.

Why the hell did she feel it necessary to put on this charade? Was his presence in her life so unthinkable that she had to go to these measures to make people believe they meant nothing to each other?

The bartender set the glass of whiskey in front of Trey and he snatched it up and took a deep swallow. He'd spent hours trying to figure out how he really felt about her, and now this. So far, the relationship had been mostly physical. But from the beginning, Trey had sensed there could be something much more to it.

All those years ago, they'd come together for one night and something had happened to him. A switch inside him had been flipped on, filling him with a sense of the man he was meant to become. And now that he was back in Belfort, with Libby so close, he felt as if he belonged here.

After he'd left for college, Trey had managed to convince himself he'd been in love with Libby. Over time, the feelings had faded. But in retrospect, Trey realized they'd never completely gone away. Was what he felt now really love, or was it the same silly infatuation he'd experienced as a teenager?

All he knew for sure was that he didn't like Libby

"dating" Carlisle Whitby. And if the gossips in Belfort were going to link one man to Libby Parrish, Trey wanted to be that man.

"I haven't seen you here before."

Trey glanced to his left to find a woman sitting on the bar stool next to him. "I haven't been here before," he replied.

"So does that mean you're new in town?"

"You could say that."

"My name's Lila. I'm not from around here."

She held out her perfectly manicured hand and Trey took it. "Nice to meet you, Lila. I'm Trey." He smiled, then picked up his drink and took a slow sip. He'd known a few women like Lila before, women who spent hours in the gym and in the salon, yet managed to look older than they really were. Her smile, her mannerisms, even her sultry drawl were trained to tease and entice. Tonight, she'd chosen to turn her charms in Trey's direction and he was glad for the distraction.

"Are you here alone?" she asked.

"Not anymore," Trey replied. He motioned to the bartender and ordered Lila a drink. After a few minutes of small talk, it was clear that Lila was looking for a lot more than just conversation. Her hand rested on his thigh and she rubbed her leg against his provocatively.

"Why don't we go somewhere a bit more private?" she suggested.

"Actually, I could use something to eat," Trey replied. Though he wanted to leave, he wasn't about to leave with Lila. And maybe being seen spending time with Lila would help with Libby's ridiculous plan to divert attention.

"We'll eat before we leave." She drained her glass of wine, then slid off the bar stool and took his arm. They walked toward the dining room, but before they reached the hostess, the door of the restaurant swung open and Libby stepped inside.

She froze, a startled expression on her face, when she saw Trey. Carlisle ran into her from behind, the door hitting him in the backside. Her gaze darted back and forth between Trey and Lila.

"What are you doing here?" she hissed.

"I heard this was a great place for dinner. Thought I'd give it a try. Libby, this is Lila. Lila, this is my neighbor, Libby Parrish." He leaned forward and held out his hand. "Hello, Carlisle. How's the mail business going?"

"Hello," said Carlisle, a suspicious glint in his eye.

Suddenly, the bar seemed to go quiet and Trey could feel the other patrons watching them all. "Now that we ran into each other, why don't we have dinner together?" Trey suggested. "Carlisle, you wouldn't mind, would you? Lila doesn't know many folks in town and I'm sure she'd enjoy meeting new people."

"Well, I—"

"Great," Trey said. "I'll get us a table." He smiled to himself as he slipped past Libby, his arm brushing against hers for a fleeting moment. He steered Lila through the dining room, his hand resting on the small of her back. The hostess showed them to a table near the windows, and Trey stepped around Lila's chair and pulled it out for her. Libby waited for Carlisle to do the same and when he didn't, Trey took the job.

But the instant she sat down, Libby jumped back up again, clutching her purse in her hands. "If you'll excuse me, I'll be right back." She hurried out of the dining room, turning back long enough to give Trey a desperate look.

"I'm just going to get another drink," Trey said. "Would you two care for anything else?" He didn't wait for an answer before heading off after Libby.

They met near the ladies' room, Libby pacing back and forth in the small hallway, her color high, her green eyes bright with anger. "What do you think you're doing?" she demanded. "And who is that woman you're with?"

"Her name is Lila. I just met her at the bar. She's real friendly, but she's not from around here."

"She's real friendly, I'm sure. You had your hand on her butt!"

"You know, you might be on to something there," Trey said, lowering his voice to a conspiratorial whisper. "If I'm seen with Lila and you're seen with Carlisle, then your plan is bound to work. By the way, how's that plan of yours going?"

"It's going just fine," Libby said. "But I really don't think it's necessary for you to participate."

"Why not? While you're enjoying yourself, I should be able to have a good time, too, don't you think?"

"A good time? Is that what you want?" She cursed beneath her breath, then spun on her heel and shoved the bathroom door open. It swung back, but Trey slipped inside before it shut.

"You're not upset, are you?"

"Get out of this bathroom. You're causing a scene!"

He glanced around. "There's no one in here but us, Libby. Who's here to see?"

"You did this on purpose. You're jealous of Carlisle and you're angry because I wouldn't cancel our date, so you came down here to spoil our evening together."

"No," Trey said, backing her up against the sink. In one effortless motion, he grabbed her around the waist and set her on the edge of the vanity. "I came down here for a drink. But now that I am here, I think I will do my best to spoil your evening." Trey hooked his finger under her chin and drew her lips to his. "Because I know you'd rather be spending the night with me."

"Don't you dare kiss me," she warned.

"I have to kiss you," Trey whispered, brushing his lips across her mouth. He slowly ran his palms up and down her thighs, pushing her skirt up higher each time. "And I think you have to kiss me, too."

Trey didn't wait for her to refuse again. His hands slipped beneath her skirt as he covered her mouth with his. She didn't resist and he tested her lips with his tongue. A tiny sigh slipped from her throat and her fingers found his nape, furrowing through his hair and pulling him closer.

Libby tipped her head back and Trey traced a line with his tongue from her mouth to her ear and then lower. He pulled her silk blouse off her shoulder and sucked gently on the skin at the base of her neck. He wanted to leave a mark, proof that he was the only one who could possess her.

His hands wandered over her body, growing more familiar with the soft curves and warm flesh. Trey tugged at her blouse and Libby followed his cue, frantically unbuttoning his shirt and yanking it from his trousers.

They touched bare skin at the very same time, their soft moans mingling. The danger of discovery was part of the thrill and in the back of Trey's mind; he wanted someone to walk in, wanted to prove that everything he'd shared with Libby was real and not just the stuff of rumors.

He pushed Libby's skirt even higher and then grabbed her thighs, pulling her against him so she could feel his need, hard and hot beneath his trousers. She locked her ankles around his waist and Trey gently leaned over her, grateful for the barrier of fabric between them. If it wasn't there, Trey would have slipped inside of her, damn the danger of discovery. But when he made love to Libby Parrish, he didn't want to do it in a public restroom. He wanted her alone, with nothing to interrupt them, nothing to keep them from exploring the real limits of their desire.

He wasn't sure how long they kissed and touched and tore at each other's clothes, but Trey was beyond caring where he was. So, when door of the bathroom swung open, neither one of them heard it. But they did hear the admonition that followed.

"Goodness gracious, this is the ladies' room, not some brothel!"

Sucking in a sharp breath, Libby pulled back and risked a glance at the door, all the while scrambling to restore order to her clothes and hair.

"Lisbeth Parrish, is that you? Who is that with you?"

Trey smiled and nodded. "Trey Marbury. Nice to meet you." He gave the elderly woman a little wave.

"If you'll give us a few seconds, we'll just get out of your way."

To his relief, the woman stepped back outside, offering them a chance to compose themselves. Trey helped Libby button her blouse and then smoothed his hands over her rumpled hair. Her face was flushed and her breath was coming in quick gasps. "I didn't hear her open the door," he murmured.

"Do you know who that was?" Libby said, stepping out of range of his grasp. "That was Charlotte Villiers. She's the biggest blabbermouth in town. Thanks to you, it's not going to be speculation anymore. By tomorrow morning, everyone in Belfort is going to know about you and me and how she found us nearly naked in the ladies' room at Tarrington's. I hope you're happy."

Trey shrugged. "I'm not happy that we had to stop. But maybe it's for the best. This really isn't the proper place for—"

"And you know of a better place? Why don't we just do it in the middle of Center Street and we'll invite the whole town? I live here, Trey, and you don't. How do you think it feels to have people whispering about me?"

"Let them whisper. I say, let's give them something to whisper about."

He tried to slip his hands around her waist, but Libby pushed him away and walked to the door. "Just go home," she ordered. "I'll talk to you later."

"What about Lila?"

"Maybe you should take her with you, if she's really what you want." She pulled the door open and walked out.

Trey turned to the mirror and stared at his reflection for a long moment. Trey should have been happy to step into the arms of a woman like Lilah—a woman so obviously interested in pleasure. But there was something about Libby he couldn't seem to resist. Since he first set eyes on her again, other women held absolutely no appeal. He flipped on the faucet and splashed cold water on his face, patiently waiting for his desire to cool.

"Maybe you should just walk away," he said as he dried his hands and face with a paper towel. But Libby was like unfinished business—or untapped potential. If he didn't stick around to explore what was possible between them, then he'd always wonder.

When Trey stepped out of the ladies' room, Charlotte Villiers was standing outside. He sent her one of his most charming grins and she couldn't help but return the smile. "I believe I might be falling in love with her," Trey whispered. "What do you think? Do you think I have a chance?"

"You could find a more appropriate place to court her than a public washroom," Charlotte suggested.

He chuckled and then strolled down the hallway. Hell, if people were going to gossip, then let them speculate about a romance between them. Because this wasn't just about sex anymore, Trey mused. He was beginning to believe that he and Libby had been meant for each other all along.

LIBBY KNEW THE PATH by heart. She could walk it with her eyes closed or in the dark of night and still find her way through the thick brush and overgrown trees. When she stepped out into the clearing, she drew a deep breath of the warm night air. Mosquitoes buzzed around her and she brushed them away as she pulled her dress over her head and kicked off her shoes.

The water was cool as she walked in and she let it lap around her body. Libby closed her eyes and sank down, then dipped her head back to wet her hair. All she wanted was to wash away every thought of Trey. She lay on her back and floated, looking up at the stars.

A few weeks ago, she'd wished for a little excitement in her life and now there seemed to be too much. Since Trey had come back to Belfort, her entire world had shifted. How could she possibly still want him after all these years?

Things between them had always been unfinished in her mind. After writing him that ridiculous letter, the ramblings of a love-struck seventeen-year-old, Libby had convinced herself that they were destined to be together. When he hadn't answered, she'd imagined him at school, surrounded by beautiful college girls with bouncy hair and perfect cheerleader figures.

Why would he have wanted to come home to a mousy high schooler who'd never been able to fill out a bra or turn a cartwheel? There had been a time when just the thought of Trey had made her feel inadequate. But now it was different.

It felt good to be pursued, to know that he wanted her now as much as she'd wanted him then. Maybe this was the way it was supposed to be. She'd make him fall in love with her, and the scales would suddenly balance and her life would make sense. Maybe then she could erase the hurt from the past.

But Libby couldn't deny she had feelings for him. The jealousy she felt when she saw him with Lila was proof of that. Just the thought of him touching another woman made her want to throttle him.

"How's the water?"

With a tiny yelp, Libby sank down in water up to her neck. She didn't have to see him to know he was standing on the shore. "Go away, Trey. Haven't you caused enough trouble tonight?"

"Not quite," Trey said. "In fact, there's a whole lot more trouble to be had now that I've found you."

She retreated to deeper water. "What happened when you and Lila left? She looked eager to please. Why aren't you seducing her tonight instead of bothering me?"

His deep voice came out of the dark, sending a shiver down her spine. "Come on, Libby, you know you're the only one I want to be with. If you need me to say it out loud, there it is." He reached for the front of his shirt and began to unbutton it. "I only have eyes for Libby Parrish."

"You're not coming in this water."

"Oh, I think I am."

"No you're not. You're trespassing. This is Parrish property and if I want you to leave, then I have every legal right to ask you."

"You can ask, sweetheart, but you don't want me to leave." He shrugged out of the shirt and started on his trousers, kicking off his shoes and socks along the way. He paused before he unzipped his fly. "We are skinny-dipping, aren't we? I'd hate to get out there and find out you're not really naked."

Libby watched as he skimmed his boxers over his

hips. She couldn't see much in the dark, but she could see enough to appreciate his broad chest and narrow hips. A soft sigh caught in her throat as he moved closer to the water. He was beautiful and so undeniably masculine. She'd seen him nearly naked on several occasions, but now, without a stitch of clothing, Libby considered him much more dangerous—and irresistible.

She felt a knot of desire twist inside of her, sending warmth snaking through her bloodstream. They'd been so close that night in her bed and even that night on his veranda. The need inside her had been building for days and she ached to touch him, to have his hands on her body, to linger over love-making as if they had all the time in the world.

He walked through the shallows, then dove cleanly into the water. With strong strokes, Trey crossed the short distance to where she stood. When he popped up in front of her, he shook his head. Libby covered her face and yelped in protest as he splashed water in her face.

"The water feels good," he said, swimming around her, his shoulders and backside breaking the surface.

"I should be angry with you." Libby bobbed away from him, unwilling to let him touch her. If he did, she'd find herself in the same situation as she had in the bathroom—out of control. Once Trey laid his hands on her, she couldn't seem to resist him.

"Come on, Lib. I'm sorry I messed up your evening. But you have to admit, dating Carlisle was kind of a silly idea."

"It would have worked if you hadn't shown up.

Charlotte Villiers would have seen me with him instead of with you, and she would have told everyone in town."

"Why is this so important to you? Why let the gossips bother you?"

Libby turned away, staring at a light across the river. "Because someday, you're going to leave and I'm going to have to live here. And I don't want to be known as the poor fool who slept with Trey Marbury."

Trey reached out and found her hand, then drew it up and out of the water. He laced his fingers through hers, then kissed the back of her hand; his lips were warm on her cool, damp skin. "I came here the first night I was in town," he admitted. "I remembered this place from that night we spent together before I left for college. I wanted to see if it was still the same."

"That night is in the past," Libby said, reluctant to talk about painful memories. "We were different people back then. We were just kids."

"Sometimes it seems like it was yesterday. And then, when I came here again and I saw you, it took me back to that time."

"You saw me?" Libby asked.

He nodded. "You were swimming. You stood right over there and took your clothes off and I thought I'd stepped into a dream. God, you were so beautiful—*are* so beautiful. I didn't realize it was you at first. Then you turned and the moon lit up your face, and I was that kid again."

"Do you ever think about that night?" Libby asked, her voice trembling slightly.

"Yeah, I do," he admitted. "A lot. I was pretty confused and you made me feel better."

"The sex?"

"I know I wasn't that great, but—"

"You were," Libby said, reaching up to smooth her hand over his cheek. "I wouldn't have changed a thing."

He bent his head and looked into her eyes. "You know, that was my first time, don't you?"

Libby bit back a gasp. "But I thought—"

He chuckled softly. "Yeah, the old expectations again. I kissed a lot of girls and we did a lot of other things. And there was a lot of locker-room talk and speculation. But the truth of the matter is, I was scared. I had a way out of this town—a way to get out from under my father's thumb—and I didn't want to do anything to mess it up."

"Then why did you do it with me?"

"Because it felt right. I honestly thought you cared about me."

"I did," Libby said. "But then you know that, don't you." She didn't want to make him feel guilty for the past, for all the hurt his desertion had caused. So much of who he was had been tied up with his family that it was no wonder he'd walked away and never looked back. And the letter she'd written him must have seemed like even more pressure.

"You were my first, Libby. And I don't think I've ever forgotten that. Just being with you, talking to you that night. You seemed to understand what I was going through. I never thanked you, but in a way, you kind of made me the man I am today."

She brushed her fingers across his lips and Trey kissed her fingertips. Though she couldn't see the subtleties of his expression, she heard the emotion in his voice. "I never really got over that night, either," she murmured. She leaned forward and kissed him, drawing her tongue along the crease of his lips.

For a long time they explored each other's mouths, their hands and lips the only point of contact. The cooling water swirled around them, gliding over naked skin and heightening sensation.

Trey slipped his hands around her waist and pulled her close, their bodies meeting beneath the water. He picked her up and pressed his lips to the base of her throat. "Neither one of us knows what's going to happen here," he whispered. "But when we're together, it feels good. Why should we deny that?"

Libby furrowed her fingers through his wet hair. "Just because it feels good, doesn't always mean it's a good idea."

He smoothed his hands along her thighs and gently drew her legs up around his waist. Libby held her breath, trying to slow the furious pounding of her heart. They were so close. If she just sank down slightly, he'd be inside of her.

"I like kissing you, Lib. And I like touching you. If you don't want me to do that, you're going to have to tell me to stop."

"I have," Libby teased. "You don't listen."

"All right," Trey said. "Tell me once more. Tell me not to touch you."

Libby opened her mouth, but Trey quickly kissed her. When he drew back, she shook her head. "That's not fair."

"What's not fair is this body of yours." He shifted slightly and Libby felt his hard shaft probe at her entrance. And then, she moved and he was inside her, the contact taking them both by surprise.

A low moan slipped from his throat as she let herself sink down on top of him. Libby froze, trying not to move; their bodies were nearly weightless in the water. She sensed he was dangerously close to losing control, but it felt so good to have him buried deep inside of her.

"Oh, God, Libby," he said, the words tight in his throat. "Don't move."

Libby shifted again, drawing herself upward, the tip of his shaft teasing at her entrance. "I won't," she murmured, kissing him again. She sank down again, tipping her head back and enjoying the sensation.

He sucked in a sharp breath. "If you keep this up, I'm not going to want to stop." Slowly, he lifted her higher until the contact was completely broken. And then, he let his tightly held breath escape. Furrowing his fingers through her wet hair, Trey dragged her into another kiss, seducing her with his tongue and his lips. And when she was breathless with desire, Trey gazed down into her eyes. "The second time we make love is not going to be in a river," he said.

"Where then?" Libby asked, her fingers drifting below the surface. She ran her fingers along the length of his shaft.

He moaned softly and then grabbed her wrist. "Let's do what I said before and get out of town," he said, his lips warm against her ear. "Let's make this about us, instead of everyone else in Belfort. I want to spend days in bed with you, Lib, and we can't do that here."

"Where?" she asked. "And when?"

Trey chuckled. "Anywhere and as soon as possible. You just let me know and I'll be there."

"I have to go to New Orleans tomorrow on business. My flight leaves at one tomorrow afternoon, Delta 762. Meet me at the airport in Charleston and we'll go together. We can stay a few extra days."

He grinned, then kissed her again, picked her up and carried her out of the water. "All right. I'll meet you there."

Libby stared into his eyes, her fingers smoothing over the planes and angles of his face. Maybe it was best that he couldn't really see her, couldn't see the indecision in her gaze. "Sometimes, I wonder if this has all happened too fast. Look at me. I'm swimming naked in a river with a man I barely know. A few weeks ago, the most excitement I had in my life was when I found an organic bug spray for my roses."

"Believe me, sweetheart. I can guarantee I'll be a lot more exciting than bug spray."

"Show me then," Libby murmured, nuzzling her face. "Touch me."

Trey growled playfully, then picked her up and tossed her into the water. He swam after her and then pulled her beneath the surface, kissing her as they sank.

They played in the water for a long time—touching and kissing, talking and teasing, bringing each other to the edge of pleasure and then dancing away. Libby could have spent the entire night in the river with him, simply to be near him.

Though they both wanted to make love, they'd reached an unspoken agreement. They walked from the water, hand in hand, and dressed each other—his hands smoothing over her body, her fingers caressing him. And when he left her at the door, he left her wanting the feel of his hands, still warm on her body, and the taste of his tongue, still damp on her lips. She thought about sneaking out and crawling into his bed, but Libby was willing to wait, knowing that when they were together again, it would be the realization of every fantasy she'd ever had about Trey.

It would happen, it would be perfect—and it would change everything between them.

6

"COME ON, BEAU, let's go." Trey opened the driver's side door to the Jeep and waited while the dog jumped inside. Then he tossed his bag on the back seat.

Though it was just past ten, he still had to put gas in the Jeep, drop Beau at the kennel outside Belfort and pick up his ticket before he met Libby at the gate. They had decided to drive separately, and she had left early that morning with Sarah to do some work at the studio before leaving for the airport.

He and Libby had barely been able to walk away from each other the night before. He'd wanted to carry her up to her bed and make love to her right then. But he wanted Libby free of inhibitions and worries, not watching the clock and waiting for dawn. And the only way to have that was to get out of Belfort.

He slid in behind the wheel and backed out of the drive. But he'd barely turned onto Charles Street when his cell phone rang. He'd given Libby the number but as he picked it up and glanced at the caller ID, Trey recognized the Chicago area code.

"Hello, Mark," he said after switching on the phone.

"When the hell are you coming back to Chicago?"

"I told you I'd be gone for a few months. It's been three weeks."

"Seems like three years. I can't work with Dave. He just doesn't understand what I need from him."

Trey glanced over his shoulder as he turned onto River Street. "Dave Sorenson is my best architect, Mark, and I trust him. You can, too. He's up to speed on all the projects and he knows if there's a problem, he can call me."

"Well, there's a problem. The Elton Place project is about to fall through because Dave can't seem to convince the client to change the site plan."

"I'll call him later today," Trey said. "We'll work it out."

"You need to get back here."

"Don't worry. I'm coming back. If the Elton project goes south, I'll drive back for a few days next week and get it straightened out."

"You *are* coming back for good, aren't you?" Mark asked. "Just tell me that you are."

"Yeah," Trey murmured. "Yeah, I'm coming back."

Even as he said the words, Trey couldn't help but wonder if they were a lie. Chicago seemed like a world apart, a place that had been easy to forget now that he'd settled into the lazy rhythms of Belfort.

He'd come back to Belfort to deal with his father's estate and to come to terms with his death, yet he'd done very little to sort out those feelings. Instead, he'd thrown himself into an affair with Libby Parrish. Was his single-minded pursuit of her just a way to avoid dealing with the guilt? Or was he truly falling in love with Libby?

Before Clayton Marbury had died, Trey hadn't seen him for almost three years. And before that, it had been even longer. After the shoulder injury in college had knocked him out of football for good, his father's disappointment had infused every conversation and argument they'd had. Trey refused to return to Belfort but he occasionally joined his parents for Christmas at their cabin in the Ozarks. And his mother came to visit him twice a year in Chicago. He had waited for his father to make the first move and accompany her north. That had never happened, and he'd died still estranged from his only child.

As Trey turned onto Center Street, he brushed aside those thoughts, choosing to replace them with the problems at work. He grabbed up his cell phone and punched in the two-digit code for his office number. A few seconds later, the receptionist answered the phone. "Hi there, Elise, it's Trey. Can you put me through to Dave?"

He waited, listening to the canned music over the line. But when he glanced in the rearview mirror, Trey noticed a police car following hard on his back bumper. Almost immediately, the cop turned on his lights. With a soft curse, Trey glanced at the speedometer and realized he'd been going at least ten miles per hour over the limit. He quickly switched off the phone, tossed it on the seat next to Beau and pulled over to the curb.

Trey watched as the officer, a burly man with dark hair and reflecting glasses, lumbered up to the Jeep. When he stood beside the Jeep, Trey forced a smile. "Mornin'."

"License and registration please," the cop ordered.

"Can I ask why you stopped me?"

"License and registration," he repeated.

Trey reached over, flipped open the glove compartment and retrieved his registration, and then grabbed his wallet from the back pocket of his pants. The officer examined both carefully, shoving the sunglasses up on his forehead as he did. Trey thought he recognized the man, but he couldn't put a name to the imposing figure in blue.

"Chicago, Illinois," the officer said. "That where you're livin' these days? Tell me, Mr. Marbury, do they ride around all day talkin' on them little telephones where you come from? 'Cause here, we pay more attention to our drivin'."

"I'm sorry, I didn't realize there was a law against—"

"Well, there is here in Belfort. Passed it just last year."

Trey groaned inwardly. "I didn't realize that."

"I'm afraid I'm going to have to take you into the station."

"Now? Can't you just write me a ticket and I'll pay the fine?"

The cop slowly shook his head. "Seein' as you're from out of state, I need to check for any outstandin' warrants."

Trey smiled and tried to remain calm. A simple infraction now looked like it would take up more time than he had to spare. Libby was waiting and they were finally going to have some time to themselves. He needed to get to the airport! "Technically, I'm not from out of state. I grew up here. My dad was—"

"I know who you are. Now, if you'll just step out of the car, Mr. Marbury. I don't want to have to cuff you."

Trey pushed open the door. This was ridiculous! "If I'm riding down to your station in your car, what am I supposed to do with my dog?"

"Well, bring 'im with," the officer said as if the answer were self-evident. "Can't leave him in the car alone, can you? Not in this heat."

Cursing beneath his breath, Trey waited for Beau to jump out of the Jeep, then locked the door and followed the officer to his squad car. "Officer, I'd—"

"It's not officer," the man grumbled. "It's chief. I'm the chief of police here in Belfort, so you can call me Chief Talbert."

"Bobby Ray Talbert?" Suddenly the face and the hulking body were familiar. Bobby Ray had played on Trey's offensive line at Belfort High. "Geez, Bobby Ray, why didn't you say it was you? How are you? Hell, I didn't realize you were in law enforcement."

"That's Chief Talbert to you," he muttered.

Trey smiled. "Right. Chief. Well, this doesn't have to be complicated. I'm not a criminal. I'm on my way to the airport and I'd be happy to sign any papers and pay any fines right up front. And I can assure you that I don't have any outstanding warrants. I'm an architect in Chicago."

"We get plenty of northerners down here runnin' drugs up from Florida," he said. "It's my job to check these things out."

Why was everyone in Belfort determined to do his or her civic duty? Trey rode the three blocks to the police station in the back of Bobby Ray's cruiser. Beau stretched out on the seat beside him and when they got to the station, Bobby Ray ushered Trey inside. Beau, who had committed no crime, was allowed to lie on a sofa while Trey got a cold metal bench in a holding room.

He glanced at his watch and mentally calculated how long it would take him to get to Charleston. If he could get out and on his way within the next hour, he'd still be able to make his flight. But as the minutes ticked by, Trey realized that the police in Belfort moved as slowly as the rest of the folks in town.

After an hour, Trey stood up and asked to use the phone, but the female officer at the desk ordered him to sit down and wait. He considered calling a lawyer, but he'd have to use his one phone call to get hold of Libby at the airport.

Sometime before one, after nearly three hours of waiting, Trey decided he'd had enough. He demanded to see the officer in charge or he'd be forced to call a lawyer. A few minutes later, Bobby Ray strolled in and sat down on the bench beside him. He handed him two tickets. "There's one there for the cell phone violation and one for speeding. You were clocked going ten miles per hour over the limit. I also have you for an unlicensed dog and a rolling stop when you turned onto Center Street, but I'm goin' to let you slide on those."

"Thank you," Trey said, pushing to his feet. "I'll just take care of these and be on my way."

"Not so fast," Bobby Ray said. "There's something else. I got a complaint about you the other day and I just wanted to let you know, I'll be keeping an eye on you, Trey Marbury."

"A complaint?" Trey asked.

"Here in Belfort we have an old law on the books that prohibits fornication between two unmarried people. I understand you've been chasing Lisbeth Parrish around town."

"Great. Now you're going to get involved in our personal lives, too? Join the crowd."

"I take a particular interest in Lisbeth. She's a fine, upstandin' citizen and a local celebrity. Plus, she's a damn fine cook. So you can see, I wouldn't look fondly on you takin' advantage of her. So watch yourself, boy, or you're going to end up back in this cell and it'll take a whole lot more than a couple hundred bucks to get you out." With that, Bobby Ray got up. "You can leave now. Y'all have a pleasant day."

Trey was forced to walk back to his Jeep, Beau trotting at his side. By the time he'd finished paying the fines and buying a Belfort license for his dog, it was well past one. He had no idea where Libby was staying in New Orleans, so when he got home, he called information for Sarah Cantrell's number.

"Unlisted," he muttered as he threw the phone onto the floor. "This is just great."

The only saving grace of getting arrested and missing his flight was that now he'd probably have the entire weekend to figure out just how he was going to explain this to Libby.

"YOU WERE GREAT," Sarah said. "I don't know why you get so nervous before these things. You're always very entertaining. That story about the grits had them rolling in the aisles."

"It did go well," Libby said. "But they didn't laugh at my gumbo joke. And I missed a whole section when I was talking about low-country cuisine."

"Well, we sold over two hundred cookbooks and

we took a bunch of orders for the new DVD. I'd call this weekend a great success."

"Yeah," Libby murmured. "Great."

Sarah shook her head as she reached for her luggage on the carousel. "You've been moping around all weekend. Would you like to tell me what's wrong?"

"Nothing's wrong. I'm just tired and I want to get home." She grabbed her bag, but it slipped in her hand and landed on her foot. Libby cursed and kicked the bag, tears welling up in her eyes. "God, I hate my luggage!"

Sarah frowned, shaking her head. "You know, this mood of yours probably has nothing to do with your luggage. I'd venture to guess that this has something to do with Trey Marbury, seeing as how you haven't mentioned him all weekend."

"I don't ever want to hear his name again," Libby muttered. "If you say it, I'll fire you."

"You can't fire me because I don't really work for you," Sarah said. "I own the production company that produces your show. Technically, you work for me."

"Well, then, you should fire me for being such an idiot."

"I generally think you're pretty smart, Lib."

Libby shook her head and she dragged her suitcase toward the door to the parking lot. "Not when it comes to men. I invited Trey to come with me this weekend. He was supposed to meet me at the airport on Friday and we were going to have a nice romantic weekend away from Belfort. We were going to have a wonderful time and I was really looking forward to it."

"What happened?"

"He stood me up. He never showed up at the airport, he didn't call. He just left me waiting there feeling like the biggest fool in the world. The same way he left me waiting twelve years ago."

Sarah patted Libby on the back. "I'm sorry. You should have told me."

"At first, I was humiliated," Libby continued, relieved to finally unburden herself. "I mean, I waited until the last minute to get on the plane. And then I got angry. I really was hoping that this weekend would…" She shook her head. "I hoped it might make things clear between us."

"He probably has a good explanation," Sarah said as they got into the elevator in the parking ramp. "Maybe something came up, a family emergency or something to do with his business. Did you check your machine?"

"I can never remember the code," Libby said.

"And he didn't leave a message at the hotel?"

"I don't think he knew where I was staying."

"Nice planning there, Lib. You invite the man away for a romantic weekend and you don't bother to tell him where you're going?"

"I don't want to talk about this," Libby said, her nerves frayed and her patience waning. She rubbed at a knot of tension in her temples. "This probably happened for a reason. We're not supposed to be together. It's…fate. Maybe I'm glad he didn't show. It would have made things more complicated and I don't need that in my life right now. The truth is, the closer we get to actually doing it, the more scared I become."

"Scared of what?"

"What if making love to Trey changes everything?

What if I fall in love with him again? I'm not sure I'd be able to watch him leave."

"I've watched you over the past few weeks and I think you're already in love with the guy."

"I am not!" Libby cried, picking up her pace when she saw Sarah's car. She waited for her friend to unlock the trunk and then threw her bags inside. "What we have is just a bad case of lust, not love."

"Right now, I don't think you can tell the difference," Sarah said.

They drove back to the station in silence. Libby tried to stop thinking about Trey, but she kept trying to rationalize what had happened. Maybe Sarah was right. Maybe he had a good excuse. But in the end, did it really make a difference?

When they got to the station, Libby put her bags in her car, then turned to say goodbye to Sarah, anxious to get home and find Trey.

"Are you going to be all right?" Sarah asked.

Libby nodded. "Sure. Hey, whatever it is, I can handle it. I'm in complete control. Well, maybe not complete, but—"

"Don't go home, then," Sarah said. "Let's get some dinner. We'll drive back together and stop to eat at that seafood place we like. You can pick up your car when we come in for the lighting design tomorrow."

The receptionist greeted them as they walked inside and then waved a sheaf of pink message slips in their direction. "I have some messages for you, Miss Parrish. This guy has been calling all weekend. He says you know him and that he was supposed to go to New Orleans with you. He asked where you were staying. I think he might have been calling for

Dewey, you know, that crazy fan who's always following you around. I recognize Dewey's voice so he never gets through anymore but—"

"Trey Marbury?" Libby asked.

"Yeah, that was his name. Do you know him?"

Libby nodded. She picked up the stack of messages and flipped through them. "Did he say anything?"

"No, just that you should call him. Oh, then the last time he called, he mentioned something about leaving town and he left his cell phone number."

"What?"

"He said he'd explain in his letter."

"What letter?"

The receptionist shrugged. "I don't know. Maybe he sent it to your house."

"Come on," Sarah said, pulling her toward the door. "I'll drive you home now."

"I can drive," Libby said as they went out. "I'm fine. Hey, I always knew he'd leave sooner or later. It's better that it was sooner, before I got too attached."

Sarah walked Libby back out to the parking lot, then wrapped her arms around Libby and gave her a hug. "I've got a few things to do here, then I'm headed home. Why don't you and I rent a movie tonight and eat two or three of those pies you keep in the freezer? We'll have a girl's night."

Libby shrugged. "I'm really tired. I think I'm just going to take a shower and go to bed early. But I'll talk to you tomorrow, all right?"

Sarah waved as Libby drove out of the parking lot and headed for the highway. "Maybe this is for the best," she repeated as she fixed her gaze on the road. "I was falling in love with him."

But admitting her feelings didn't seem to mitigate the pain and regret. Would it take her another twelve years to get over Trey Marbury? Or would she spend the rest of her life wondering what might have been?

THERE HAD STILL been no relief from the heat wave after another week and a half. Every window in Libby's house had been thrown open to catch even the slightest breeze. People on the street talked about the weather forecast in great detail, praying for rain. Libby had taken to wearing the lightest cotton dress she could find and forgoing underwear if she wasn't planning to leave the house.

The only time she had a moment's relief was when she stood in front of the refrigerator or the air conditioner that rumbled in her bedroom window. Beyond that, she tried to stay still as she could and take a cooling shower whenever the heat became especially unbearable.

Libby peered out the screen door at the house across the street. It was Thursday afternoon and the bridge club was in full swing in the Throckmortons' front parlor. No doubt, the subject of today's conversation would be Trey Marbury's hasty exit from Belfort.

The breeze teased at her hair and she stepped out onto the front veranda to enjoy it while it lasted. Her gaze drifted over to the house next door. Contractors had been hard at work there, and she'd heard through the grapevine that the guys in charge regularly spoke to Trey. But she hadn't heard a word since he'd left.

Libby sat down in one of the wicker rockers and pulled out the letter Trey had left in her mailbox.

She'd taken to carrying it in her pocket so she could read it whenever she felt the need. Libby had hoped that she might find something in his words that would tell her she'd made the right decision, that putting Trey firmly in her past was the only course of action.

She slipped the letter out of the envelope and unfolded it, then slowly read the words again.

Dear Libby,

I'm not sure I can explain the events that conspired to keep me from making our flight and it probably doesn't make a difference. If you're angry with me, then my explanations won't matter. Maybe missing that plane was a good thing. It gave me some time to think and I realized that I've been pushing you toward something I'm not sure you're ready for. Now, I have to leave and I'm hoping this will give you time to decide what you really want. I'll be back soon. But I do know that we're going to have to either finish this once and for all—or start planning a future together. I'm sorry if I messed up your life here and if my return has caused you more pain than our time together was worth. But I didn't want to walk away again without telling you that you have and always will own a part of my heart.

Take care, Trey

P.S. If you want to talk, you have my number.

Libby stared at the note for a long time, the words blurring in front of her eyes. Her anger at Trey had dissolved over the past ten days and now she felt only a dull ache in the vicinity of her heart. She missed him. But Libby had to admit the distance had given her perspective. She'd come to realize just how deep her feelings were for Trey.

It wasn't about lust and it wasn't about control anymore. She wanted to surrender to him, completely and utterly, and forget about the repercussions. She couldn't be happy unless she let herself love him—even if it was for just a little while.

She reread the text, but as her gaze scanned each line, Libby realized that something had been bothering her about the letter, something nagging at her mind. And it had nothing to do with the sentiments expressed. She walked back inside the house, heading directly to the kitchen.

Trey's first note was still in the drawer beneath the microwave. She'd been afraid to take it out, afraid that the erotic words might bring back feelings she wasn't prepared to deal with. But as she laid the two side by side on the table, the problem became clear.

"Oh, God," she murmured, her eyes darting back and forth between the two letters. The handwriting on the first looked nothing like the handwriting on the second! So if Trey had written and signed the second, then who had sent her the first?

"Carlisle?" Libby murmured. She moaned and then covered her eyes. But she'd mentioned the letter to Trey that night before she'd tied him up on his veranda. And he hadn't questioned her about it. "What man would ask questions in a situation like that?" she reasoned. "He wasn't thinking with his head, he was thinking with his…"

Her cheeks warmed and she drew a deep breath, trying to make sense of her chaotic thoughts. Outside, a dog barked; the sound grated on her nerves. With a soft curse, she snatched up the letters and walked to the back door. At the same moment, Beau bounded up on the veranda. Libby screamed in surprise and then realized if Beau was home, so was Trey.

She pressed her palm to her damp forehead, then frantically combed her hair with her fingers. Trey was nowhere to be seen, but she knew he wouldn't be far behind. She needed a shower and a dress that didn't look like she'd slept in it.

Libby raced through the house to the stairs, but she was only halfway up when a knock sounded on the back door. She stopped in her tracks.

"Libby?"

She drew in a quick breath at the sound of his voice. Her heart began to race and for a moment, she forgot to breathe. She turned for the kitchen and then decided that she couldn't face him looking like a wreck. In the end, Libby just sat down on the stairs, too confused to move.

The screen door creaked and she heard footsteps echo through the house. "Libby?" She tried to stand, but her knees were weak. She wrapped her fingers around the balusters and waited. A few seconds later, Trey wandered into the entry hall.

"Libby?"

"Hi," she murmured.

He circled the newel post and sat down next to her. "I'm back," he said, staring at her with a perplexed expression.

"Yes, you are."

"I wasn't sure whether I should come over," Trey said.

"It's all right. I would have brought Beau back."

"That's not what I meant. I wasn't sure that you'd want to talk to me. You didn't call."

"I thought it would be good to give it some time," Libby said. "You were right. We needed a chance to take a breath."

He reached out and took her hand, weaving his fingers through hers. In truth, she wanted him to pull her into his arms and kiss her senseless, to erase every last doubt from her mind. His absence had only made her realize that her life seemed empty without him in it.

He stroked her face, his gaze moving between her eyes and her lips. "I missed you, Lib. I drove all night to get back here." He brushed his mouth across hers, his tongue tracing the crease of her lips.

Libby wrapped her arms around his neck and lost herself in the taste of him. She lay back on the stairs and he stretched out over her, deepening the kiss until desire overwhelmed her. When he drew back, he smiled at her, smoothing his fingers along her cheek. "God, I almost forgot how beautiful you are." He pushed to his feet and pulled her up along with him. "Come on," he said, pulling her up the stairs.

When they reached her bedroom, he pulled her down on the bed and slowly began to undress her. "Wait," Libby said, shaking her head.

"Wait?"

"I need to know about this," she said, holding out the letter she still clutched in her fingers.

He sat up. "I figured I should at least say goodbye," he murmured. "I tried to call you, Lib, but I couldn't find you. And then Mark called from work and I had to go back."

"And this," she said, holding out the other letter.

He frowned. "What's that?"

"I got it in my mailbox the day after you came to me, the night of the storm. I thought it was from you, but the handwriting doesn't match."

Trey scanned the note. "Wait here," he said, crawling off the bed. He hurried downstairs and Libby heard the screen door slam behind him. She lay back on the bed and tried to slow her pulse. Had she known of his return, she might have been able to steel herself against these feelings. But she felt as if she'd been ambushed by her own desire.

A minute later, Trey rejoined her upstairs, handing her a letter as he sat down. "Whoever wrote that one, wrote this one, too. The handwriting is the same."

Libby scanned the contents of third letter, her eyes widening as she read. "You thought I wrote this? That's why you came to me that night?"

"And this is why you came to me a few nights later," he said. Trey chuckled. "It seems someone is playing a little game with us."

"Who?"

"Does it really matter?" Trey asked, nuzzling her neck.

"Of course it does."

"Why? Letters or no letters, I think what happened between us would have happened anyway. We had unfinished business, Libby. Maybe that's why I decided to stay here in Belfort or why you automatically thought that the letter was from me."

"And now it's finished?" Libby murmured.

"Not by a long shot." His gaze searched her face. "As far as I'm concerned, it's just getting started."

Libby drew a ragged breath. "But sooner or later, you're going to leave again. And I'm going to have to get used to life without you next door. Without you in my bed."

He opened his mouth and then snapped it shut again. "What do you want from me, Libby?"

She bit her bottom lip to keep from answering truthfully. What she really wanted was for them to live happily ever after. She wanted to grow old with him in Belfort, raising a bunch of kids and spending their lives madly in love with each other. But Libby knew that the chances of those wishes actually coming true were slim to none. "I want time," she said. "Time to figure out what this all means and what I should do about it. I thought I knew what I was doing, but I didn't."

He furrowed his hand through the hair at her nape and pulled her closer, pressing a kiss on her forehead. He lingered there for a moment and Libby prayed that he wouldn't wander down to her lips.

"Then take the time," he murmured. "When I make love to you, Libby, I want you there, body and soul." He crawled off the bed and handed her the letters, then smiled down at her. "I'll see ya, Lib."

"See ya, Trey," she said.

Libby drew a ragged breath and sank back into the pillows, throwing her arm over her eyes. She'd bought herself some time, but what good was it going to do? The simple fact was, she wanted Trey. As long as he was living next door, she'd want to talk to him and touch him, kiss him and share her body with him.

Libby crawled off the bed, grabbing up the three letters. "I am such a coward," she muttered. She'd seduced him when she was seventeen. She was a grown woman now and she was more insecure than she had been back then.

"It's nice to know that I've actually regressed in my sex life," Libby muttered.

7

THE OFFICE WAS located in a small brick building on River Street. Trey had called his father's secretary and asked her to meet him there at noon with the keys. Though he'd been putting off going through his father's business effects, Trey figured it was something that had to be done sooner or later. The building would have to be put up for sale before he could think about heading home.

"No one's been here for months," Eloise said as she unlocked the office door. "I think your father kept the office because of me. You know, he paid me my full salary, even though all I really did was collect rent and deposit the money in the bank account. The tenants could have mailed the money directly to him, but he was very generous that way."

"I've heard that about him," Trey murmured.

Once he walked inside, Trey wasn't sure whether he really wanted to be there. As a kid, he used to spend Saturday mornings at the office with his father, anxious to please and starved for the attention. But sometime after he had reached the age of twelve, Trey had begun to rebel, chaffing at the expectations his father had of him.

Football became the focus of his life from the time

he'd entered high school and it was something that was all his—until his father intruded on that as well. Trey's mother always used to tell him that Clayton Marbury's meddling was the way he showed his love. But it never felt like love to Trey. It felt like punishment.

"I've boxed up all the files," Eloise said. "But I didn't touch anything in your father's office. I thought that was for the family to do."

"Thanks," Trey said.

"There are some extra boxes in the corner." Eloise patted him on the shoulder. "I'm sorry about your father, Trey. He was a good man."

"Thanks," Trey repeated, now numb to the expressions of sympathy.

She handed him the key and then left him alone with the task and his thoughts. Trey drew a deep breath and slowly walked through the reception area toward his father's office. He'd thought about hiring someone to do this job, but then realized it might help to deal with the memories straight on. That's why he'd taken time from work to come back home, so that he could get everything clear in his head.

The blinds were pulled and the interior of the office was warm and stuffy. Trey crossed to the huge windows and threw them open to the light and the fresh air. This had been his father's entire life, the work that he'd loved, the hub of his little empire. At least Trey could understand that passion. He felt the same way about his own work.

He took in the space—from the abundance of natural light, to the high ceilings, to the vintage details. The office would be perfect for an architect, with plenty of wall space for sketches and blueprints. But then, he wasn't going to consider staying in Belfort unless he had a reason to stay. And right now, his only reason was keeping her distance.

Trey sat down in the huge leather chair and tipped his head back, closing his eyes and letting more memories flood his brain. He'd never really taken the time to pinpoint when it had all gone so bad with his father, when they'd stopped talking to each other and retreated into anger. But he did remember happy times as a boy—tossing the football around on a Sunday afternoon, driving to Atlanta for a baseball game, fishing off a pier in the river.

"Hey, there."

Trey opened his eyes to find Libby standing in the doorway. He couldn't help but smile at the sight of her. She wore a pretty flowered dress and her hair was pulled up in a haphazard ponytail, strands of blond caressing her cheeks. They hadn't spoken in three days and he'd begun to wonder if he'd ever see her again. "Hey, Lib."

"I saw you come in here," she said. "I thought you might want some company."

"How is it you know exactly how I'm feeling? My own father, whom I lived with for years, never had a clue what was going on in my head." Though he'd decided to give her space, that didn't mean that he'd stopped thinking about her. If anything, his attraction to her had intensified. There was just something about Libby. She understood him like no one else ever had.

"I guess I'm just really smart," she said with a coy smile.

"Yes, you are," Trey replied. "And very beautiful, too."

She crossed the room and circled the desk. "So this is your dad's office," she murmured, taking in all the details. "Headquarters of the evil empire?" Libby smiled ruefully. "We used to drive past here when I was a kid and my father always had something nasty to say. He usually put a curse on the place. You're lucky he didn't know any real voodoo."

Trey chuckled softly and he reached out and captured her hand. He pressed a kiss to her fingertips. "That feud. I don't even know when it started. My parents used to talk about it all the time, but I never paid attention."

"The Throckmortons know all the details," Libby offered. "If you're really interested I'm sure they'd be happy to fill you in. It had to do with one of my relatives getting shot in the butt by one of your relatives."

He pulled her down on his lap and grinned. As long as she was here, he wasn't going to let the opportunity slip by. "I think you and I have pretty much put an end to the hostilities. Why don't we declare an official ceasefire right now?"

She stared into his eyes, then brushed a quick kiss over his lips. "Deal," she said.

Touching her again felt good, Trey mused, her silken skin, her delicate fingers. She'd driven him wild with those hands, with that mouth, with her body. He wondered how he'd ever be able to touch another woman again without thinking about what he'd shared with Libby. And in that instant, he realized he didn't want any other women.

"So, are we kissing again?" he asked, pressing his lips to her bare shoulder. "Because if we aren't, I'd like to know so I don't make an ass of myself."

Libby pushed off his lap and wandered over to the shelves behind the desk, refusing to answer his question. She picked up a photo of Trey in his football uniform. "You used to be such a babe," she teased.

"Right," he muttered, laughing as he spoke. "That's all padding. I was a pretty skinny guy."

"You've filled out nicely. I was so in love with you back then, skinny legs and all."

Trey spun around in the chair and then reached up to rest his hands on her waist. He leaned forward and pressed his forehead against her belly. "I'm glad you're here. I miss you, Lib. I'm not sure why this is so difficult, but it's easier now that you're here with me."

Libby gently ran her fingers through his hair, the action calming him. "You and your father had a lot of issues and you were never able to get past them. Maybe you regret that you didn't try hard enough."

"I didn't try at all," Trey admitted. "And I should have. God, Libby, I don't want to spend the rest of my life keeping that resentment all bottled up inside me. For a long time, I hated him. And then, I just felt sorry for him. And now I realize that, despite everything, he was still my father and he was just looking for a way to love me."

"I think your father wanted you to grow up to be a good man. And he was trying his hardest to make sure that happened. He just didn't know how to do it the right way." She bent down and kissed the top of his head. "But he succeeded because he did raise a good man."

He looked up at her, emotions welling up inside of him. "So you were in love with me?"

"I was a very silly girl with some very strange romantic ideas," she said, brushing a lock of hair off his forehead. "But I've grown up now."

Trey wondered what it would take to get Libby to love him again. Because he wanted to tell her exactly how he felt, wanted to say those words to her before it was too late.

"I should get some boxes," she murmured. Libby slipped out of his grasp and went outside to the reception area. When she returned, she began packing away the items on the shelves behind the desk, then paused when she came upon a large book. She laid it on the credenza and opened it. "Look at this," she said.

"What is that? An atlas?"

She shook her head. "It's a scrapbook."

Trey stood behind her, his chin resting on her shoulder, his arms wrapped around her waist. Libby flipped through the pages, each of them covered with newspaper clippings. His father had saved every mention of Trey in the newspapers, from the time he'd played in his first junior varsity game to all the articles about his shoulder injury at Tech. "I can't believe he kept all this stuff."

"It's obvious he was very proud of you," Libby said. "If he wasn't, he'd never have kept a book like this."

Trey turned her around in his arms, his gaze fixed on her beautiful face. How was he supposed to stop himself from kissing her or touching her? Over the past weeks, he'd almost taken the opportunities for granted, but now… "Oh, hell," he muttered.

He quickly cupped her face in his hands, searching her wide green eyes for a clue to her feelings. Then he bent close and kissed her, softly and gently, lingering over her lips, tracing a line with his tongue. "If you don't want me to kiss you, then you'd better tell me to stop," he murmured against her mouth.

"Don't stop," Libby said, her palms smoothing over his face.

"Why was it we decided we shouldn't be together? I forget."

"I needed time to think about all this."

"And have you thought about it?" Trey asked. "Because it's all I've been thinking about, Libby. And I just want to stop thinking and start feeling again."

She shook her head. "Trey, I—"

He pressed a finger to her lips and forced a smile. "I'll try not to kiss you. But, hey, you're welcome to kiss me anytime you want."

"I'll keep that in mind."

As Trey helped Libby pack up the rest of the books, he watched her move around the room. How the hell had he walked away from her that first time? He'd been too young and too stupid to realize what she'd offered him. And now that he'd had a second chance at it, he'd managed to screw it up somehow.

He wanted Libby to want him the way that he wanted her, with a need that bordered on irrational. He didn't want to have to hold back, to restrain his desire and wait for her to kiss him. He wanted her in his arms when he fell asleep at night and when he woke up in the morning, and he wasn't going to settle for anything less.

They worked through most of the afternoon, and for the first time, Trey had a chance to see another side of Libby. She was sweet and funny and open, and organized to a fault. They talked more about his childhood and his problems with his father and by the time they finished packing up the office, Trey felt as if he'd worked through some of his guilt.

He'd also come to realize that he was in love with Libby Parrish. Trey had never really understood what his married friends saw in a lifelong commitment to one woman. But after spending the afternoon with Libby, he could visualize a life with her, with a woman who understood his deepest fears and insecurities. But his experiences with women in the past had left him completely unprepared to make a future happen with Libby.

"That's it, then," Trey said, staring at the stacks of boxes.

"What are you going to do with all this?" Libby asked.

"Put it in storage, I guess. Until all the properties are sold, I suppose we'll have to keep it. The personal stuff I'll send to my mother."

"Well, I should go then," she said. "I've got some work to do at home."

Trey reached out and took her hand, lacing his fingers through hers. He drew her fingers up to his mouth and placed a kiss on her wrist. "Thanks for your help. I owe you dinner. Or a cake, or something."

"No problem," Libby said, smiling winsomely. She took a deep breath and pulled her hand away to rub her palms on her skirt. "Well, I'll see you, then."

"Right," Trey said, fighting an urge to pull her into his arms again. "I'll see you."

He watched her walk to her car from the office window. A rumble of thunder rolled in the distance and the sky was growing dark with clouds. The breeze freshened and suddenly shifted direction. Trey closed the window, then took one last look around the office. He'd put some things to rest today. He'd be able to leave his problems with his father in the past and move on with his life—a life that he hoped might include Libby Parrish.

As he jogged down the steps and walked outside, the wind began to buffet the trees along River Street. He ran to his Jeep and hopped inside, then pulled out into traffic. A moment later, the first raindrops splattered on the windshield.

Trey thought about the last time it had rained. He'd spent that night in Libby's bed, sneaking away in the early morning light. He flipped on the wipers as he turned onto Hamilton Street. Wind-whipped leaves swirled on the pavement and lightning flashed overhead as images of that night whirled in his brain.

He pulled into the driveway a few minutes later and drove to the old carriage house that served as a garage. A storm like this often brought hail, so he pulled the Jeep inside and ran for the house. At the last minute, he decided to check on Libby, to find out if she'd put her car inside. He knew it was a feeble excuse, but Trey didn't care.

As he cut through the azalea bushes, he saw Libby standing in the middle of the back lawn, her face turned up to the sky, her arms outspread. Her cotton dress was soaked and clung to her body as the rain dripped off her fingertips. Trey watched her for a long moment, stunned by her beauty, and then slowly started toward her.

Perhaps she sensed his presence or perhaps she'd had enough of the cooling rain. But when she opened her eyes, she looked directly into his gaze. He froze and they watched each other for a long time, both of them weighing the consequences of what they were about to do. And then, as if the rain had washed away the last traces of indecision, they walked into each other's arms.

Trey tipped her damp face up to his, covering her mouth and drinking in the taste of her. Their kiss turned frantic and he moved from her mouth to her cheeks and her eyes and her forehead, the rain cool on his lips, her skin warm.

They didn't have to speak, to verbalize what they both felt; it was there in every breath, in every sigh. They needed each other and, suddenly, all the rest of it didn't matter.

Trey scooped her up into his arms and carried her across the lawn. When they reached the shelter of the veranda, he set her on her feet again and kissed her, this time whispering her name over and over again. He would have been satisfied to leave her there, knowing that this might be all she wanted. But Libby took his hand and drew him inside, letting the screen door slam behind them.

They slowly walked up the stairs to her bedroom, the rain pounding on the roof and hissing on the hot pavement outside. The thunder of the storm obliterated all thoughts of the outside world. He'd been waiting twelve years for this, searching for a woman like Libby and never finding her.

And now, as they walked toward her bedroom, Trey realized that there was no other woman for him. There never had been. From the first moment he'd touched her, he'd fallen in love with Libby and now that he'd found her again, he had every intention of spending the rest of his life with her.

HIS HANDS SKIMMED over her body and Libby tipped her head back as Trey kissed her neck. Why had she even bothered to deny this need? Now that she'd given up the fight, Libby could only feel relief. She would take her pleasure from Trey and count herself lucky that they'd managed to find each other again. She'd worry about the rest later.

Her dress and hair dripped water around her feet. Trey moved lower and then cupped her breast. His warm mouth fixed over her nipple, the nub pushing against the wet fabric, a wave of sensation racing through her. Libby moaned, furrowing her fingers through his hair.

Frustrated by the barriers between them, she pushed him away and reached down for the hem of her dress. She yanked it over her head. At the same time, Trey shrugged out of his shirt, tossing it aside. Libby reached for the button on his shorts, but he caught her wrists.

"Before this goes any further, I have to run back to my house. I forgot something there."

Libby pressed her face into his chest, the light dusting of hair tickling her nose. "You don't have to," she said.

"Lib, we can't—"

"No." She smiled up at him. "The last time I was in Charleston, I took care of that. Although Harley and Flora Simpson might be angry, I took my condom business elsewhere. I thought it best to be discreet."

He wrapped his arms around her waist, pulling her body against his. "Good girl. This is Belfort, after all, and we wouldn't want to start any gossip." With a low chuckle, he steered her toward the bed. Trey stared into her eyes, gently brushing the damp strands of hair from her forehead and temples. "Are you sure you want this?" he asked.

Libby smiled. "I haven't ever stopped wanting it." She hooked her fingers around her panties, then slowly slid them over her hips and along her legs before kicking them aside. Then she reached over to Trey and stripped off his shorts and boxers, allowing her hand to brush against his growing erection.

His breath caught in his throat as she walked to the bedside table and retrieved the box of condoms. Libby handed them to him and he tossed them on the bed, then tumbled them both onto the four-poster.

She expected him to seduce her quickly, but Trey had other ideas. He roamed over her body, his lips exploring sensitive spots, his hands running along her limbs and torso. Libby closed her eyes and gave herself over to experience, letting him have his way with her, surrendering completely to the experience.

He pressed a kiss against her instep, then slowly worked his way upward. But this time, Trey stopped, his mouth trailing along her inner thigh. Libby held her breath and in a heartbeat he was there, his tongue parting her and finding the sensitive heart of her desire.

He teased and tasted, drawing her along with him until Libby's fingers were twisted in the sheets and her body arched against him. "Trey," she murmured, his name on her lips the only link left to reality. His tongue slipped inside of her and Libby cried out, a wave of pleasure washing over her. She felt herself teetering on the edge, but then, as if he could sense her excitement, Trey brought her back down.

He braced himself, levering up from the bed. "I want to feel you come. I want to be inside you when that happens." Trey reached over her to retrieve the box of condoms, then tore open one of the foil packages and handed it to Libby.

But Libby set the condom aside and began her own exploration of his body. Her lips found familiar spots on his neck and his chest, then teased at his shaft before moving on. His body was perfect, lean and hard, his skin smooth.

Everything that had happened between them, from that very first argument in her rose garden, had led to this. Somehow, time had collapsed and she was here with the boy she'd loved all those years ago. But he wasn't a boy anymore. He was a man who knew what he wanted and right now, he wanted her.

Libby picked up the condom and slipped it out of its package. Trey braced his arms behind him and watched as she drew it over his shaft. He held his breath and tipped his head back, a lazy smile curling his lips.

"What do you want?" Libby asked, letting her fingers drift along his rigid desire.

"I want you," Trey replied.

Libby pressed her hand against his chest and pushed him back into the pillows, then straddled his hips. She moved against him, his shaft pressed against her moist entrance. And then he was inside her, penetrating just slightly at first. Libby arched her back as she slowly sank down on top of him, burying him to the hilt.

He grabbed her waist and held her still for a moment. Libby remembered the first time they'd done this, how clumsy and awkward and unnerving it had been. But now, it seemed like the most natural thing in the world, to share this intimacy with Trey, to invite him inside her body.

"Slow," he murmured, loosening his grip on her waist.

Libby smiled and pushed up on her knees, then slid back down over him. "That slow?"

Trey growled. "You're bent on torturing me, aren't you?"

She moved again, this time sinking deeper. "I believe I am."

Trey reached between them and touched her, gently rubbing his thumb against her sex. "Then I'll have to return the favor."

Libby smiled, drawn into his little challenge and determined to emerge victorious. But as she moved above him, the tension inside her began to build and her thoughts became more focused on the waves of pleasure coursing through her body, centered on the touch of his fingers where they were connected.

He brought her close again, only this time she picked up her pace, leaning over him and kissing him deeply. Her hair fell around her face and his breath came in shallow gasps as their lazy lovemaking began to take on an unrestrained edge.

Trey murmured softly against her lips, urging her forward. And then, suddenly Libby was there, her body tensed and her nerves tingling. She gasped as the first spasm hit her, then cried out as exquisite sensations overwhelmed her body. She kept moving, driving him deeper until his hands clamped down on her hips and he found his release. The pleasure seemed to go on forever, her limbs going numb, her nerve endings alive.

And when it was over, she began to move again, very slowly, drawing the last shudder out of him. He groaned and then rolled her over beneath him, their bodies still joined. "I'm not even going to ask how you got so good at that."

"What I lack in experience, I make up for in enthusiasm," Libby teased. "That, and I read a lot of books."

They lay in bed for a long time, wrapped in each other's arms and listening to the storm outside. And when they were ready, they made love again, Trey stirring her desire and possessing her body like no man ever had.

As Libby stared up into his eyes, his hips nestled between her legs, she realized that she could spend a lifetime caught up in this passion. Now that she had him in her bed, she never wanted to let him go.

But deep in the most secret corner of her heart, she knew there'd come a time when her bed would be empty and her body unfulfilled. When that time came, Libby vowed to remember this moment, with him moving inside her, his handsome face suffused with pleasure. That would be what she'd live with and Libby was satisfied it would be enough.

A COOL BREEZE WAFTED through the room, the curtains billowing out from the windows. Trey opened his eyes to the early morning light, then snuggled up against the slender body beside him bed. He sighed softly, nuzzling his face into the curve of Libby's neck.

The rain had continued for most of the night, finally breaking the heat wave that had oppressed the area for weeks. The air smelled fresh and green, and the birds sang more vigorously in the live oaks.

He reached up and smoothed a strand of hair off her forehead. They'd been awake until just before dawn, talking and making love, then talking some more, all the years apart providing fuel for their conversation. He'd anticipated that when it finally happened between him and Libby, it would be like his wildest fantasy. And now that it had happened, he'd been proven wrong. Making love to Libby had been so much more than a fantasy.

It hadn't just been about pleasure, although the sex had been incredible. He'd made love to this woman for only the second time in his life, and it had felt totally and perfectly right. They belonged together—he knew it as he moved inside her, as he watched her pleasure increase and as she shuddered in his arms.

Trey found the symmetry of their relationship almost poetic. He'd never believed in love at first sight, but that's what had happened with Libby. It had just taken them a little time to find each other again. And now that they had, he didn't plan ever to let her go.

"Hey, Lib," he murmured, brushing a kiss across her lips.

"Umm?"

"Are you awake?"

She slowly opened her eyes. "I am now." Yawning, she drew her hand over her eyes. "What time is it?"

"I don't know. Probably close to eight. Maybe even nine. I thought maybe I'd go out and get us some breakfast."

She wrapped her arms around his waist and nestled into his body. "No, don't leave. I'll make breakfast. Or lunch. Or we'll have pie. I have apple pie in the freezer."

"All right. Pie sounds good. Can we eat that in bed? Now that I've got you here, I don't want to let you leave."

Libby sat up and brushed her hair out of her eyes, tugging the sheet up around her naked body. "I have to go to Charleston today. We're going to do a test taping of the show. We have to see how the new set and lighting look before we start taping next week."

Trey groaned. "You have to go?"

"I do," Libby said, leaning over and kissing him softly. "But I'll be home by seven or eight. We could have a late dinner."

"Then you're thinking you might want to see me again?" Trey asked. "This isn't just a one-night stand?"

She shrugged, then smiled coyly. "Yeah. Maybe we could try this again."

"And you're not worried about the gossips anymore?"

She giggled and then rolled on top of him. "Not so much. I'm doing exactly what I want to do and if they want to waste their time speculating about it, they can. They'll never really know how good it was anyway." She wriggled against him and Trey felt himself growing hard again. "After you make love to me again, maybe we should go out for breakfast."

Trey rolled her beneath him and gazed down into

her eyes. "I think we might want to wait on that, Lib. At least until you've had a chance to talk to the chief of police."

"Bobby Ray Talbert? Why would I want to talk to him?"

"He's the reason I didn't get on that plane to New Orleans."

She frowned. "What?"

"He hauled me into the police station on some trumped-up charges and then he told me if I continued seeing you that he'd arrest me again. I don't think he cares for me too much. He seems to have a crush on you."

"Bobby Ray Talbert asks me out twice a year," Libby explained. "Fourth of July and New Year's Eve."

"Maybe you should go out with him," Trey teased, "so I don't end up in jail."

"What you did to me should be against the law. It felt too good to be legal."

"According to Chief Talbert, it is against the law here in Belfort. Unless we're married, of course. Then it would be perfectly legal." He paused. "Maybe we should get married."

He kept his tone light and teasing, as if he were merely joking. But in truth, Trey wanted to see her reaction, to test her feelings for him. Had she ever considered a future with him? Was marriage completely out of the realm of possibility?

Her brow furrowed into a frown, then she laughed. "Right. With you in Chicago and me in Belfort? Trey, you don't have to make me any promises. And you don't have to feel as if you owe me anything. I know you're going to leave sooner or later, and I'm all right with that. We'll enjoy the time we have together and that will be enough."

Trey stretched out beside her, his arm braced against the pillow. "What if it's not enough for me?"

She fixed her gaze on his, as if trying to read the sudden shift in his mood. "What are you saying?"

Trey saw a flash of panic in her eyes and he chuckled softly. "Nothing. It's just…I'm going to miss you when I leave."

She brushed a kiss across his lips. "I'll miss you, too." Libby tossed aside the sheet and crawled out of bed, then grabbed her robe from the chair near the window. "So what do you want for breakfast? I can make waffles or pancakes. Eggs and grits. We can have biscuits and gravy."

Trey grabbed her hand as she passed the bed, yanking her down on top of him. "Right now, I'd settle for a few more minutes of you."

But as he kissed her again, Trey knew it was a lie. A few more hours, a few more days, would never be enough. He wasn't about to settle for less than a lifetime.

8

LIBBY MOANED SOFTLY as she opened her eyes. The sun had come up long ago but for the fifth morning in a row, she and Trey had decided to sleep late. There didn't seem to be enough hours in the night for them. She rolled over and snuggled against Trey's body, slipping her arm around his waist.

They'd fallen into a routine of sorts. By day, Trey spent his time overseeing the renovations next door, stopping by to share lunch with her if she wasn't at the station in Charleston. Later in the evening, they'd have dinner, the meal filled with conversation and good food, laughter and wine, as they recounted the events of the day. But they usually found one excuse or another to turn in early and then their night would begin, a long night of lovemaking.

Nestled in the curve of his arm, Libby kissed his shoulder. She'd grown accustomed to having him in her bed, his hair dark against her pillow, his limbs draped possessively over her body. It felt…right.

Libby knew it would be foolish to allow herself to depend on him. Trey had a career and a life in Chicago. When it was time for him to leave, she'd be devastated. But her affair with Trey had been exactly what she needed, a reminder that her life was there to be lived if only she was willing to take a few risks.

There would be other men, she told herself. Maybe not as wonderful or exciting as Trey. Though he was her first love, she had to believe he wouldn't be her last. She looked at his face, the features so familiar to her now, and a wave of emotion washed over her.

Tucked away, deep in her heart, a tiny glimmer of hope had begun to grow. Maybe there was a chance for them, slim as it might be. She didn't want to believe it, but she couldn't help herself. Libby had always been too romantic for her own good.

She pushed the thoughts out of her mind and carefully slipped out of bed. After grabbing her robe, she wrapped it around her naked body and then curled up in the chintz chair by the window. Beau had taken to sleeping in the chair, enjoying the benefits of a second home and a lenient hostess. But he was stretched out in front of the door and barely lifted his head to greet her.

Libby tucked her feet beneath her and watched as Trey slept, memorizing each feature of his handsome face. Some day, she'd want to remember the tiny scar on his chin or his impossibly thick lashes or his sculpted mouth. Someday, that would be all she had left, an image of him she kept locked away in her mind.

Trey stirred, then reached out to the empty spot beside him. When he didn't find her there, he sat up, rubbing the sleep out of his eyes. "Hey," he said.

Libby smiled at him. He looked so boyishly handsome in the morning, his hair all mussed, his eyes half-hooded. "Hey, yourself."

"What are you doing up?"

Libby shrugged. "Just watching you sleep."

He reached out his arm toward her and crooked his finger. Libby pushed out of the chair and crawled back into bed beside him. He pulled her up against his body, tucking her backside in the curve of his lap. "God, I love waking up with you."

"That's because I always make you breakfast," Libby murmured, slowly stroking his arm.

He rested his chin on her shoulder. "That's not true. And to prove it, I'll make you breakfast this morning. What are you hungry for?"

"Can you even cook?" Libby asked.

"No, not very well. I can make toaster waffles and I'm pretty good with cereal. I once tried French toast, but that was a disaster. I figure if I make an effort, you might offer to help."

"Do you want eggs and bacon or pancakes?"

"Yes, please," Trey said. "And I'd really love some of those biscuits you make. Maybe with some honey?"

Libby kissed his arm and then sat up, resting her chin on her knees. "I think we used all the honey last night. I'm going to have to wash the sheets, they're so sticky."

The doorbell rang and Libby groaned. Beau jumped up and barked, but Trey called him over and ordered him to lie down beside the bed. "Who'd be ringing the bell at this hour?" she muttered.

"It's probably Carlisle. I don't know why he has to hand-deliver your mail." Trey sat up and tossed the sheet aside. "Let me go down. I'll get rid of him."

Libby yanked him back onto the bed. "Don't you dare. I suspect he might have been the one to complain about you to Bobby Ray Talbert. I don't need him running over and telling the chief of police that you and I have been fornicating."

"Is that what we were doing?" Trey teased. "Can we do it again?"

Libby slapped at his hand as she slipped out of bed. "No, not now." She adjusted the belt on her robe. "I'll be back in a second."

The doorbell rang again and Libby raced down the stairs and pulled the front door open. But Carlisle wasn't waiting on the porch with a package. Instead, Libby found Bobby Ray Talbert waiting, his hat clutched in his hands. His face was flushed and he shifted nervously, back and forth, from one foot to the other.

"Mornin'," he finally said in a strangled voice. "I—I mean, mornin', Miss Lisbeth."

Bobby Ray always turned into a blithering wreck whenever she was within ten feet. "Good morning, Chief Talbert."

He laughed uneasily, his gaze dropping to his feet. "You can call me Bobby Ray," he murmured.

Bobby Ray usually preferred to approach her at the grocery store or the post office. He'd never once been brave enough to climb the front steps of her porch. "What can I do for you, Bobby Ray?"

"I was just over next door, lookin' for Trey Marbury. He's not home. You wouldn't know where he was, would you?"

"Now why would you think I'd know?"

Bobby Ray shrugged. "There—well, I'm not one to take gossip seriously—but, you know, there have been rumors floatin' 'round town."

"I'm surprised you're listening to gossip, Bobby Ray. Don't you law enforcement officers usually focus on facts?"

"Well, yeah…most times. But there are cases when a—a rumor might be just as helpful." He turned his hat over in his hand and idly brushed a speck of lint from the crown. "Would you mind if I came in? There's a few matters I'd like to discuss with you. Maybe you and me could have a glass of lemonade?"

Libby glanced over her shoulder. Could she really refuse the chief of police? If she did, Bobby Ray was bound to get suspicious and he was a stickler for the law. The last thing she wanted was for him to haul Trey out of her bed and charge him with fornication.

"All right," she said. "But I'm not dressed. Maybe you could walk around back and I'll join you there in a few minutes with a cool drink."

He nodded, a wide smile breaking across his face. "Well, fine then. It's a date." His smile faded. "I—I mean, not a date date. Not that I wouldn't mind a date…date. It's just that lemonade isn't…well, that's not what I meant."

"I understand, Bobby Ray. And I'll meet you out back in a few minutes."

"Take your time," he said, backing toward the steps.

Libby waited until she heard his footsteps on the side veranda. Then she raced back up the stairs, nearly tripping as she rounded the landing. She found Trey still lying naked in bed, his arm thrown over his eyes, the sheet tossed aside. "You have to get up," she whispered. She crawled over the bed and shook him hard. "Trey, get up."

Trey moaned, then rolled over on his stomach. "Did you get rid of Carlisle?"

"It wasn't Carlisle. It's Bobby Ray Talbert. He's waiting on the back veranda. I'm supposed to bring him lemonade."

"Good," Trey said. "I love your lemonade. I could use a glass of something cool. You think he wants to join us for breakfast? Maybe he could cook."

"You have to leave," Libby whispered. "And take Beau with you."

"Come on, Lib. I thought we'd spend the day together. I don't have any contractors at the house. I've got the entire day free." He grabbed her waist and pulled her back into the bed. "I'll do very nasty things to you if you let me stay."

"You can't! The chief of police is downstairs. Now get dressed and then wait a few minutes and sneak down the stairs. Go out the front door. I'll keep Bobby Ray on the back veranda until you're gone."

"Damn it, Libby, I'm not going to sneak out. Why don't you just tell Bobby Ray and Carlisle and the rest of the folks in town to mind their own business?"

"This is neither the time nor the place to argue about privacy issues."

"This is the perfect time," Trey teased.

"And what am I supposed to say? 'For anyone who cares, I am sleeping with Trey Marbury. He does unspeakable things to me in bed and I actually enjoy them!' After my announcement, I could answer questions, kind of like a press conference. Then they can slap the cuffs on you and lead you into jail."

"Maybe I should tell everyone that I'm the guy

who has every intention of making an honest woman out of Lisbeth Parrish."

"Don't be silly," Libby said.

"I'm dead serious," Trey countered.

"And what is that supposed to mean? Are you planning to marry me?"

"I don't know. Would you consider marrying me?"

Libby looked around for her dress on the floor and waved it at him. "This conversation is getting more ridiculous by the minute."

"Answer me, Libby. I want to know where you see this relationship going."

"I'm supposed to be asking the questions like that and you're supposed to be evading the answers." She untied the belt to her robe and let it drop to the floor. Then she shrugged into her dress and ran her fingers through her hair.

"Damn it, Libby, I'm tired of you dancing around the issue. I want to know where the hell I stand. Is this just about sex? Or is there something more here?"

"Gee, it's funny you should ask that. Because that's what I was asking myself twelve years ago. Was that first time, down at the river, just about sex?"

"Of course it wasn't."

"Well, you had a funny way of showing it." She picked up his shirt and tossed it at him.

"Me? I'm the one who wrote you six letters. And you never answered one."

"You're lying."

"Why would I lie about something like that? Libby, I thought our night together was incredible. When I got to Atlanta, I couldn't think about anything else. And when you didn't write back, I thought you didn't care so I stopped writing. I didn't come home because I didn't want to run into you. Seeing you again would have been too painful."

"I wrote you a letter. You're the one who never wrote to me. Don't lie to me, Trey."

"I'm not. I never got a letter from you, Lib. If I had, I would have come home the very next weekend. I wanted to see you again."

Libby shook her head, pressing her fingers to her temples. "We don't have time to figure this out right now. Just get dressed. I'll come over later and we'll talk."

Trey reluctantly crawled out of bed and picked up his jeans from the floor. He pulled them on without bothering to put on his boxers. "You know, Bobby Ray Talbert does not have jurisdiction over our love life."

"We have no love life," Libby said. "We have a sex life. That's normally not a permanent situation. We don't have to burden the people of Belfort with the incredible details of what goes on in my bedroom."

Trey grinning. "You think it's incredible?"

"You're missing the point. I just need you to stay on your side of the bushes until things cool down with Bobby Ray."

"Hell, nobody enforces those laws anymore. I'd like to see him arrest me."

"Just go home," Libby insisted.

"How am I going to be able to sleep without you?"

"Try. Close your eyes and it'll come to you."

"I'll come to you tonight, after Bobby Ray is tucked safely into bed," Trey said.

"No!"

"Then you come to me."

"No!"

She hurried out of the room and back down the stairs. Peeking through the kitchen window, she checked on Bobby Ray, then grabbed a pitcher of lemonade from the refrigerator and a pair of glasses from the cupboard. Libby pushed the screen door open with her backside and hurried over to the pair of wicker chairs.

"It looks like it's going to be another hot day," she murmured as she filled his glass.

"Folks 'round town get a little testy with this heat," Bobby Ray commented. "Yesterday, I warned Eudora Throckmorton about crossin' in the middle of the block and she hit me with her purse. I could have arrested her. That's a 243, assaulting a police officer. I let her go with a warning."

"That was very kind of you," Libby said. "Now, why don't you tell me why you stopped by? Did I do something wrong?"

"I hope not," Bobby Ray said. "Let's call this a preventative visit. I understand that Trey Marbury is a handsome, sophisticated city boy now and some women in this town might find that type attractive. I've heard the rumors."

Libby stifled a groan as she raked her hands through her tousled hair. She found a sticky spot at the nape of her neck and winced. How had she managed to get honey back there? "You know how the gossips are here in town. They'll say just about anything to make a story more interesting."

"I'm not going to let him run around stirrin' things up."

"Stirring things up?"

"Yeah. Stirrin' women up. We have an ordinance in Belfort prohibitin' fornication between two unmarried people. Granted, the ordinance was passed in 1889, when some hookers from Charleston showed up at one of the local taverns. But still, a law is a law, and I intend to enforce that law." He paused. "If you know what I mean."

"Do you really think that law is fair?"

He stared at her for a long moment. "It's there to protect the citizens of Belfort—and that includes you." He guzzled down the rest of his lemonade, wiped his lips with the back of his hand, and pushed to his feet.

"And what if two unmarried people are in love?" Libby asked.

Bobby Ray blinked in surprise. "In love? Are you in love with Trey Marbury?"

"No!" Libby said, shaking her head. "I was just posing a hypothetical." She cleared her throat. "That's a 'what if' situation."

"Right," Bobby Ray murmured, nodding his head. "Well, I don't think the ordinance says anything about love bein' an exception to the rule. I'd still have to make an arrest." He adjusted his hat, then pulled out his sunglasses and slipped them on. "There are people in this town who care about you, Miss Lisbeth. You live here and he don't. I'm gonna do what I can to make sure you don't get hurt. That's my job." He gave her a quick nod. "Have a nice day, now, ya hear?"

With that, Bobby Ray strode across the veranda and disappeared around the corner of the house. Libby sat back in her chair and released a shaky breath. This was crazy! It wasn't just the gossips anymore; now law enforcement was poking into her personal life. Libby pushed out of her chair, cursing softly as she walked back inside the house.

Was sex with Trey worth getting tossed in jail? She moaned, then raked her fingers through her hair. "Yes," she murmured. "Absolutely."

But it wasn't just about sex anymore. And her question to Bobby Ray hadn't been purely hypothetical. What if she was in love with Trey? Libby wandered through the house, then climbed the stairs, mulling over the possibility. She'd tried so hard to keep herself from falling in love, but when it came right down to it, she'd probably fallen in love with him that day in the rose garden. Or maybe she'd never fallen out of love.

But love meant total surrender, tossing aside all her fears and risking her heart. It also meant a wedding and a long happily-ever-after. When she reached the second floor, she turned toward her bedroom, then changed her mind and walked to the attic door.

The stairs were dusty and steep. Libby crossed to the windows and threw them open to let the stifling heat escape. She used to play in the attic as a child, dressing up in the old clothes that had been packed away in the boxes. She pulled an old sheet from the top of a cedar chest and lifted the lid. Inside, carefully packed with tissue paper, was her great-grandmother's wedding dress. When she'd been little, she'd decided that one day she'd walk down the aisle wearing that dress.

Libby carefully withdrew the dress and held it up in front of her. But as she pulled the skirt from the chest, a small stack of letters scattered on the floor. Frowning, Libby gathered them up, draped the dress over her arm and headed for the stairs.

When she reached her bedroom, she carefully laid the dress across the bed and then sat down at the foot to examine the envelopes. There were five or six smaller letters addressed to her with no return address. But it was the larger envelope that caught her eye. She gasped as she recognized the handwriting as her own.

"Oh, my God," she murmured, her gaze skimming along the address. She drew her thumb over the stamp, then stared at the words printed below. "Insufficient postage."

She shuffled through the rest of the envelopes, six letters written by Trey and addressed to her. They'd been opened. And her letter to Trey had been returned by the post office. A single first-class stamp hadn't covered her ten-page missive.

The only way they could have ended up in the attic was if her mother had placed them there. If her father had found the letters, she would have been punished immediately. No, this was definitely the work of her mother.

Libby clutched the letters to her chest and drew a ragged breath. This changed everything. Trey hadn't deserted her all those years ago. Maybe he had even loved her. She'd been so quick to accuse him of lying earlier that morning.

The new revelations spun around in her head. If he cared about her back then, maybe she did have a chance at a future with Trey. Maybe he'd been the right man all along. The *only* man for her.

TREY STROLLED OUT to the back veranda, stretching his arms above his head to work the kinks out of his neck. He'd been refinishing floors all day long and his arms ached from fighting the floor sander for eight straight hours.

He brushed the dust out of his hair and then bent down to give Beau a pat on his head. The dog was curled up on the veranda, choosing the quiet spot over the noise of the sander.

He glanced over at Libby's house and saw the kitchen light was still on. Trey wandered across the yard and stepped around the bushes, anxious to see her. He found her sitting in one of the wicker chairs on the veranda, the light from the back door illuminating her profile.

He stepped closer. "So, are we safe?" Trey whispered. Libby jumped slightly, as if he'd startled her. It was then he saw the tears glittering in her eyes. "Hey, what is it?"

He crossed the distance between them in short order, taking the steps two at a time. Trey bent down in front of her, capturing her hands between his. "Libby, tell me. You're crying."

Libby brushed the tears away and shook her head. "No, I'm not."

"Come on, don't worry about Bobby Ray Talbert. I'm not going to let him arrest us."

"That's not what I'm upset about. I—I was just looking at these letters," she said. She handed him a small stack of envelopes and he stared at them, confused. "Do you remember those?" Libby asked.

Trey examined them closely in the light filtering out from the kitchen, immediately recognizing the handwriting and the return address. "I wrote these to you from college. I thought you said you never got them."

"I didn't. My mother must have kept them from me. And here's the one I wrote to you. It was ten pages long. See, I didn't know to put enough postage on it, so it came back and she kept it."

"Why are you crying?"

"Because we lost so many years," Libby said.

"No," Trey said, shaking his head. "No, you can't think of it that way. Libby, if I *had* gotten this letter, I might have come back to Belfort and we might have tried to see each other. But sooner or later, our parents would have found out and forced us apart. Back then, we weren't strong enough to fight them and we probably would have gone our separate ways. We came back together at exactly the right time for both of us." He drew her into his embrace and stood, pulling her up along with him. "I don't regret what happened back then. I'm falling in love with you, Lib. Right now."

"I think I'm falling in love with you, too," she murmured.

He hadn't expected to say the words, but they'd just come out. And now that they had, Trey knew there was absolute truth in them. He stepped back and looked down into Libby's face. Her tears had turned to a tiny smile. Trey chuckled. "I think that was a pretty important moment there."

"I guess it was," Libby said.

"So what does this mean?"

She pressed her nose into his chest and shrugged. "I'm not sure. I've only been in love once in my life. I'm not sure how it's supposed to feel."

"Whoever he was, I'm glad he wasn't able to see what a great woman he had."

Libby took the letters from his hand and held up the thick envelope. "Read this," she said. "Then you'll understand." She took his letters and pressed them against her heart. "I'm going to keep these. They were beautiful letters, Trey."

"So where do we go from here?" He kissed her forehead, inhaling the scent of her hair. God, he hated not being able to touch her the way he wanted, not being able to crawl into bed next to her and hold her all night long.

"You're going to have to go back to Chicago soon. Let's see where we are then."

"Are you going to tell your parents about us?"

She shook her head. "Not right now. We don't need to figure out the rest of our lives right this minute, Trey. Let's just see where this goes."

Though she'd said the words, Trey sensed that she wasn't really sure about her feelings yet. She still kept something in reserve, a piece of her heart that she refused to offer. And until he had captured every ounce of her love, Trey couldn't count on a future with Libby. "I'll never hurt you. I promise."

She smiled. "I think I finally believe that."

Trey nodded and pulled her into another hug. "All right. That's a start." He furrowed his hands through her hair, then tipped her face up to his. "Come on. Let's go take a shower and then crawl into bed and make love all night long."

"We shouldn't," Libby said. "The last thing we need is Bobby Ray throwing us both in jail. I need to find out if he really plans to enforce this law before we actually commit another crime."

"I'll get up early and leave before Bobby Ray gets

up. Or you can come to my place and I'll send you home before sunrise." He paused as he saw the pained expression on her face. Guilt cut through him. He was pushing her too hard and she was backing away again. "All right, I'll go home and sleep with Beau. But he doesn't smell nearly as good as you do and he has hairy legs."

Libby giggled, then pushed up on her toes and kissed him again. "We could take a swim before we go to bed," she suggested. "Fornicating might be against the law, but skinny-dipping isn't."

"I think I'd like that." Trey tossed the letters onto the chair, then took her hand and pulled her down the steps. But she stopped him in the middle of the lawn and threw her arms around his neck.

"It's all too complicated," she said. "We should just sleep together and force the issue. Make Bobby Ray arrest us and throw us in jail."

Trey knew that her desire for him had overwhelmed her common sense and she'd probably regret her actions in the end. "We'll figure it out as we go along," he said, scooping her up off her feet and carrying her across the lawn. "You know, we still don't know who sent those two other letters."

Libby smiled. "I really don't care. As you said, they brought us together—that's all that matters."

When they reached the river, they quickly tore off each other's clothes and waded into the water. And later, after he'd kissed Libby good-night at her back door, Trey sat in his kitchen and read the letter she'd written him twelve years ago. His mind wandered back to the words she'd voiced earlier that evening, that she'd loved only one other man. After reading her letter, he realized he was that man. But he was a boy back then, still finding his way and wondering what life held for him.

Now he knew. He wanted to marry Libby Parrish. He wanted to make a life with her and start a family, to create something special. He wanted to be a devoted husband and a good father, and he was willing to do whatever it took to make that happen.

He just hoped that Libby would forgive him for his methods, because he didn't want to wait another second for their life together to begin.

THE DOORBELL RANG just as Libby finished mixing a piecrust. She'd found a new recipe for a Black Bottom pie she wanted to test and include in the new cookbook. She grabbed a dish towel and wiped her hands, then turned to see Sarah rushing into the kitchen. Her friend was waving a copy of the newspaper in her hand.

"Did you see this?" she asked. "It's yesterday's paper."

"I saw it," Libby said. "I haven't read it. Other than obituaries and softball scores, there's never much in the *Belfort Bugle*."

"There is in this issue, and everyone in town is talking about it."

"Oh, no," Libby said. "Don't tell me they've started printing gossip in the paper now. Trey and I have been very careful since Bobby Ray paid me a visit last week. I have to say, the sneaking around makes it even more exciting. By day, we pretend we don't know each other and by night…well, it makes things very intense."

"You're not going to have to pretend anymore. Item number five under new business for the city council agenda. Discussion of the repeal of ordinance 321.7."

Libby frowned. "Fornication?"

"Fornication," Sarah repeated. "And guess who brought the matter before the city council."

"Trey Marbury?"

Sarah nodded. "I drove past city hall and there's already a line. The Ladies' Auxiliary from the Baptist Church is selling lemonade and cookies outside and there are pickets on the sidewalk. This is the most exciting thing to happen in Belfort since Kitty Foster left a naked mannequin in the window of her dress shop."

Libby tossed the dish towel on the counter and smoothed her hands over the front of her dress. "I guess we'd better get down there."

By the time they reached city hall, the spectators had already begun filing inside. Libby stood on her toes as they entered the meeting room, trying to see over the crowd. She saw Trey standing near the front. He looked so different from the sleepy, tousled-haired man she'd sent from her bed that morning. His hair was neatly combed and he'd shaved. He wore his business suit and a silk tie, a stark contrast from his usual baggy shorts and bare chest.

She pushed through the crowd, worked her way to the front of the room and then tapped him on the shoulder. "What are you doing?" she whispered.

"Hey there, Lib. I'm glad you're here. I can use all the support I can get."

"Why should I support this? My personal life is about to become public debate."

Trey reached out and grabbed her hand, lacing his fingers through hers and then pulling her into a quiet alcove near the fire exit. "I figured if they wanted us to play by their silly rules, then we'd just have to change the rules." He bent close to kiss her, but Libby shook her head.

"This is not some game," she said. "This is my life we're talking about. The minute you stand up and oppose this ordinance, everyone is going to know why."

"Come on, Libby, they already know. This whole town has known our business since the day I moved back. I want to be able to enjoy our time together, don't you?"

He idly stroked her arm and for a moment, the sensation distracted her. She swallowed hard. "And the only way you can enjoy it is if we can fornicate freely in Belfort?"

His lips curled into a devilish smile. "Well…yeah. Maybe. If I want to spend the night with you, I shouldn't have to sneak out of your bed before dawn. Hell, last night, Bobby Ray was parked in front of my house until 11:00 p.m. And he was there again this morning at six. He's determined to catch me and one of these days I'm going to oversleep."

"Please," Libby said. "Just drop this, Trey. Come home with me and we'll figure out another way. We can always fornicate out of town if we have to."

Trey shook his head. "I'm not leaving, Libby. I'm here for a reason. This law should have been off the books years ago."

"This is ridiculous! I can't support you on this."

She spun on her heel and walked to the back of the

room where Sarah had saved her a seat. "He's determined to go through with this."

"Trey looks really good in a suit," Sarah murmured, leaning closer. "I mean, he has the whole rugged carpenter thing going for him, but that suit makes him look completely yummy."

Libby rolled her eyes and sighed.

A gavel sounded and the crowd in the room quieted. "This meeting of the Belfort city council will come to order." Sam Harrington, president of the council, surveyed the room and then whispered something to the other four members; they all nodded. "Due to the size of the crowd, we're going to get right to the matter at hand so you can all get home for lunch. I'd assume most of you are here about ordinance 321.7, prohibiting fornication between unmarried individuals. Mr. Marbury, present your case."

Trey cleared his throat as he walked to the front of the room. "Council members, most of you know me. I spent the first eighteen years of my life in Belfort and I recently bought property here, so I feel I have a right to oppose this ordinance on the grounds that it infringes on personal privacy as guaranteed by the Constitution."

An elderly man stood up. "There's nothin' in the Constitution that gives single folks the right to mess around! I didn't have that freedom when I was young, why should you?"

The rest of the crowd began to shout and Sam Harrington pounded on his gavel until the room was silent again. "Reverend Arledge, let's hear your views on this."

The Baptist minister stood up. "Repealing this ordinance is a test of the moral foundations of our town. What kind of message are we sending to our youth if we say that premarital or extramarital sex is acceptable? I would strongly urge the council members to uphold this law."

"How long has it been since this law was enforced?" Trey challenged. "We all know that there's illegal sex going on in town. Either fully enforce the ordinance or take it off the books. But be prepared to have a jail full of fornicators."

"Chief Talbert, when was the last time the police made an arrest under this ordinance?" Sam Harrington asked.

Bobby Ray stood up. "That would have been in 1923, sir," the chief answered.

"Miss Eulalie. You have something to add?"

The elderly woman stood up, her handbag tucked neatly beneath her arm. "Although I'm a God-fearin' Baptist, I agree with Mr. Marbury. This is a constitutional issue. I'm not sure I want Bobby Ray Talbert standin' in my bedroom every night."

The crowd broke into peals of laughter and Libby couldn't help but grin. The thought of Miss Eulalie even having a sex life was too outrageous to ignore. Or perhaps it was the image of Bobby Ray and Miss Eulalie engaged in compromising behavior in her bedroom that people found so amusing. Sam banged his gavel to restore order.

"She's just interested in the additional gossip," Sarah whispered. "More illicit sex means more to talk about with the bridge club ladies."

"I have a question to pose to Mr. Marbury." Bobby Ray Talbert turned to the crowd. "If he's talkin' about premarital sex, as an officer of the law, I don't have a problem with that—as long as he takes the marital part just as serious as he takes the sex part."

"There's a good point!" Carlisle Whitby cried. "Let's see him answer that."

"Yes," Reverend Arledge said, jumping back to his feet. "I'd like to know if Mr. Marbury has considered marriage as an answer to his...problem."

"Mr. Marbury?" Sam and the council turned their attention back to Trey. "Has that thought ever crossed your mind?"

Trey turned around to look at the crowd, his gaze finding Libby's and holding it. "It has. I'm not sure she'd accept my proposal. She still has doubts about my feelings for her."

"That's easy for him to say," Wiley Boone shouted. "But can he prove his intentions are honorable?"

Trey reached into his jacket pocket and withdrew a small velvet-covered box. He slowly opened the box and held it out to the crowd. They all—Libby included—gasped at the sight of the large diamond ring inside. "I'm still hopeful she'll come around. That's why I bought this ring."

The entire crowd turned around to stare at Libby. She felt her face flame with embarrassment. Everyone was waiting for her to say something! But what was she supposed to say? Was Trey actually proposing to her? In front of all these people?

She glanced over at Sarah to find tears gleaming in her best friend's eyes. Libby drew a steadying breath and then slowly stood up. "I—I have a question for Mr. Marbury. I'd like to know his views on long-distance marriages. After all, he does live and work in Chicago. Would he expect this…potential wife to follow him or would he consider staying in Belfort?"

The crowd turned their attention back to Trey. A tiny grin quirked at the corners of his mouth. "I think I could be persuaded to stay in Belfort. I have a nice house here, and this is where I grew up. The woman I love lives here. Why would I want to leave?"

The meeting room fell silent as everyone waited for Libby's response. Sam Harrington cleared his throat. "I think we've gotten a bit off topic here." The crowd didn't agree as they simultaneously shushed him. He rolled his eyes and then nodded to Libby. "Do you have a response to that, Miss Parrish? If not, we need to get back to the agenda."

Libby swallowed hard, her heart hammering in her chest. "I—I don't have a response because I wasn't asked a question."

"Mr. Marbury, do you have a—"

"Oh, for goodness sake, Sam," Eulalie Throckmorton scolded. "Can't you just hold your tongue and stay out of this?"

"Sorry, Miss Eulalie," Sam muttered. "Please, continue."

"I do have a question," Trey said, "but I don't want to ask it until I can be sure of the answer." He slowly circled the crowd as he moved down the center aisle of the meeting room, his eyes fixed on Libby, the ring clutched in his hand.

"You're going to have to ask the question, before I can give you an answer," Libby said, stumbling over a few spectators to get to the aisle.

When they finally stood in front of each other, Trey

reached over and caressed her face with his hand. She closed her eyes at his touch, the crowd fading away right along with her doubts. "You really want me to do this here?" he murmured.

"I think you should finish what you started," Libby replied, her eyes skimming over his handsome features.

Trey chuckled softly. "All right, here it comes." He dropped down to one knee and grabbed her hand. Then he cleared his throat and spoke in a voice that carried throughout the meeting room. "Libby Parrish, I've been in love with you for years. I didn't realize it until I came back to Belfort. And now that I have, there is no way I ever want to leave you again. If you agree to marry me, I promise to spend the rest of my life loving you, and that alone will make me the happiest man in the world. Will you marry me, Libby?" He let go of her hand, took the ring from the box and then held it out to her as he waited for her reply.

She didn't even have to think before she replied. Emotion welled up inside of her as she realized she couldn't imagine her life without Trey in it. "Yes," Libby murmured, her eyes filling with tears of happiness. "Yes, Trey Marbury, I will marry you."

He slipped the ring on her finger, then stood and drew her into his arms. He kissed her, so passionately that he stole Libby's breath away. The townsfolk in the meeting room leapt to their feet and began to clap and shout and whistle their approval. Trey wrapped his hands around her waist, then picked her up and spun her around. Libby held fast to his shoulders as she looked down into his eyes.

"You'd really stay in Belfort for me?" she asked.

"Sweetheart, there never was a choice. From the moment I saw you again, I knew this is where I belong. In your life, in your arms, in your bed. And in your heart."

9

"I CAN'T BELIEVE he did this. Of all the underhanded, rotten things Bobby Ray Talbert could have done on my wedding day, this has got to take the cake."

"Are you sure he actually arrested Trey?" Sarah asked as she pulled up in front of the police station.

"Trey called me on his cell phone from the back of Bobby Ray's police cruiser. He told me to bring money for bail, so I assume he's been arrested." Libby shoved open the car door and struggled to climb out of the front seat, her great-grandmother's wedding gown tangling around her legs. She held up the skirt, then brushed the lace-edged veil out of her eyes. "I swear, Bobby Ray will live to regret the day he messed with my happily-ever-after."

"Libby, just calm down. Bobby Ray is still chief of police in Belfort. Sassing him might just put you in a cell right next to your bridegroom's."

Sarah opened the lobby doors of the police station for Libby and then pushed the train of her gown inside as she followed her. "You know, Bobby Ray did have a teensy little crush on you. Maybe he's jealous that Trey is walking down the aisle with you instead of him."

Libby turned on Sarah, her anger at Bobby Ray

bubbling over. "I love Trey and he is the only man for me and what Bobby Ray thinks about our relationship doesn't matter. If I don't marry him today, I'll marry him tomorrow! And I'll send Bobby Ray the bill for twenty pounds of crab claws."

When they got inside, Sarah grabbed Libby's hands and pulled her to a stop. She reached up and gently straightened her veil, then forced a smile. "You look beautiful."

The anger dissolved from Libby's face. "So do you. I'm so glad you're my maid of honor. I couldn't have planned this wedding without you."

"As your maid of honor, I'm going to give you one piece of advice. When all else fails, cry. Tears can be a very persuasive strategy when dealing with men like Bobby Ray," she said.

Libby nodded, then turned and walked through another set of doors into the reception area of the police station. The officer on duty gasped in surprise when he saw her approach in her wedding gown.

"Can I help you?"

"I want to see Chief Talbert. Tell him Libby Parrish is here to fetch her bridegroom." She tapped her foot impatiently, then glanced back at Sarah who waited on the other side of the doors.

"So, you gettin' married or are you married already?" the desk officer asked.

Libby sent him a withering look. Then she picked up her skirts and walked past the desk toward the offices. "Bobby Ray Talbert, get out here!"

"Miss, you can't go—"

A few seconds after that, Bobby Ray lumbered out of his office, a powdered sugar doughnut clutched in his fist. A few seconds later, Wiley Boone and Carlisle Whitby appeared in the door behind him.

Libby stared at the trio in disbelief, her hands hitched on her waist. "I can't believe this," she muttered. "Did you three conspire to ruin my wedding day, or was this all Bobby Ray's idea? I want to see Trey right now." She brushed past the trio to the heavy iron door that served as the entrance to the holding cells. When she pulled on it, it refused to open. She glared at Bobby Ray, who hurried over to unlock it. "You have no right to hold him."

He frowned, his face turning red. "I'm the police chief in this town and I can pretty much do what I want."

"What's his bail?"

"Well, that hasn't been determined yet."

"I want to see him," Libby said. "Right now."

Bobby Ray opened the door and allowed her to pass, then followed her back to the cells. When Libby glanced over her shoulder, she saw that Carlisle and Wiley had tagged along after the police chief. Libby found Trey sitting in the first cell, dressed in his tuxedo.

He stood the moment he saw her, a slow grin replacing his pensive expression. "God, Lib, you look beautiful."

She paused and smiled. "Thank you." Reaching through the bars, she cupped his face in her hands and pressed a kiss to his lips. Then she turned on Bobby Ray. "Unlock this cell. I want to give my fiancé a proper kiss."

Bobby Ray did as he was told and Libby rushed inside the cell and threw her arms around Trey's neck. "I'm going to kill Bobby Ray," she murmured as Trey covered her mouth with his.

"Not if I get to him first."

Libby glanced over her shoulder. "What's his crime?"

"Well, I haven't really charged him yet. As soon as I locked him up, he refused to answer any of my questions."

"You have to charge me or let me go," Trey said. "Our wedding is supposed to start in a half hour and considering all the work Libby has put into this, I wouldn't want to mess it up if I were you."

"He don't have to do anything," Wiley piped up. "He's the police in this town."

"If you're arresting Trey for fornication, then you're going to have to arrest me, too," Libby said. "Because the last time I checked, it's really hard to fornicate all by yourself." Libby stepped out of Trey's embrace and held out her hands. "Maybe you'd better cuff me," she said.

Bobby Ray's face flushed beet red. "I—I just brought him in 'cause I wanted to have a little talk. Then Wiley and Carlisle here started eggin' me on and it turned into a big old mess."

"What did you want to talk to Trey about?" Libby asked.

Bobby Ray shrugged, his gaze fixed on his footwear. "I wanted him to know that if he ain't good to you, then I'm goin' to make his life a pure kind of hell. You're just about the sweetest girl I ever knew and I don't want to see you gettin' hurt, that's all."

Libby opened her mouth to chastise Bobby Ray, then snapped it shut. The man had such a look of dismay on his face that she felt sorry for him. She'd never realized that Bobby Ray's feelings ran so deep. "This wedding is what I want, Bobby Ray," she murmured, placing her hand on his arm. "I love Trey. I fell in love with him when I was seventeen, while you were chasing Mary Beth Warniman around town. And I want to marry him—preferably today."

"You goin' to treat her right?" Bobby Ray asked Trey.

"I am," Trey said. "And if I don't, you're welcome to throw me in jail."

Libby sent Trey a silencing glare. "Bobby Ray, if you let Trey out of this cell right now, then I'd be prepared to offer you a guest spot on my cooking show. You'll be more famous than the governor. You can make any recipe you'd like." Libby paused, waiting for her offer to be fully appreciated. "I understand you make a mean shrimp boil. We've never done a shrimp boil on my show."

"I'm told I make a good she-crab soup, too," Bobby Ray said.

"We'll make whatever menu you'd like," Libby said. "And I want to tell you that I have a lot of nice single women who watch my show who'd be very interested in a man who knows his way around a kitchen. Why, I bet you'll get stacks of fan mail. Especially if you wear that uniform."

"I'm known for my ribs," Carlisle said. "I'm sure your viewers would be interested in my secret sauce."

Wiley frowned. "I can't hardly boil an egg," he muttered.

"It's either Trey or the shrimp boil," Libby said. "Take your pick."

"Leave him in jail," Wiley said.

"I'd take the shrimp boil," Trey suggested.

Bobby Ray glanced back and forth between Libby and Trey. "All right," he replied. "I'm thinkin' that would be the best way to go."

Libby pushed up on her toes and gave Bobby Ray a kiss on his cheek. "Good choice. Now, can we please leave? We've got a wedding to attend."

Bobby Ray stepped aside, pulling the cell door open as he did. "I'm sorry I put you in jail. I just wanted to make sure Miss Lisbeth would be happy."

Trey clapped the police chief on the shoulder. "That's all right, Bobby Ray. I suppose that's all part of your job protecting the citizens of Belfort."

The chief nodded. Trey grabbed Libby's hand and hurried her out to the street. Sarah was waiting in the car, the engine running. "I'm sorry about this," Libby said to Trey. "I wanted our wedding day to be perfect."

Trey pulled her to a stop and gave her a kiss. "Sweetheart, someday we'll tell our grandchildren about the day the police chief threw their grandfather in jail for trying to marry their grandmother. It may rival that story about Lucius Marbury shooting Edmond Parrish in the behind."

Libby pressed her finger to her lips. "Don't you dare bring up that silly feud around my father. I had enough trouble getting him to come to this wedding. I don't want anything else to go wrong today."

"Your wish is my command," Trey said, staring down into her eyes, a devilish grin quirking his lips. "I love you, Libby."

Libby looked up at Trey, then threw her arms

around his neck and kissed him. "And I love you, despite your criminal tendencies."

"Sometimes, I wonder at the luck that brought us together."

"It wasn't luck," she said and smiled coyly. "I know who wrote those letters."

"You do?"

"I found the exact same handwriting on one of our RSVP cards. And you'll never believe who it was."

"Are you going to tell me?"

Libby shook her head. "I have to save a few secrets for the wedding night."

With a playful growl, Trey picked her up and spun her around, her veil floating in the warm summer breeze. "Then let's get married, Libby Parrish. Before I manage to break another one of Belfort's laws."

"That's a fine idea, Trey Marbury." Libby placed her hands on his cheeks and gave him a long kiss. "The sooner I marry you, the sooner this town can start talking about someone else."

Epilogue

"WHAT IS GOING ON across the street?" Charlotte Villiers asked.

Eulalie Throckmorton stepped over to the front parlor window and looked out at the trucks parked in front of Libby Parrish's house. "I'd expect they're here to pick up the tent. Don't you know? The wedding was last weekend. Trey Marbury and Libby Parrish tied the knot. Engaged and married all in one month. She claims it wasn't a shotgun wedding, but I can't help but have my suspicions."

"I don't understand why they had it outside," Charlotte said. "Especially with this heat." She fanned herself with her hand and then took a sip of her iced tea.

"It was a very small wedding," Eudora explained. "Lalie and I were invited, since we were responsible for getting them together—although I don't believe they're aware of that fact. We plan to tell them on their first anniversary."

"I heard her father refused to come," Charlotte said.

"At first he wasn't happy at the prospect of a Marbury in the family," Eudora explained. "But Lisbeth's mama convinced him. She had a change of heart about the Marburys. Carolyn Parrish and Helene

Marbury are lookin' forward to the grandbabies, the first generation of Marburys and Parrishes who won't be at each other's throats."

"How is it that you got them together?" Charlotte asked.

"Well," Eulalie said, "it was all my idea. We started with a letter. A very erotic letter, mind you. And that got the ball rollin'."

Eudora sat down on the chair opposite Charlotte. "Oh, but tell her about the research, Lalie. We went to that adult bookstore on the interstate south of Walterboro. My goodness, that was an experience. We picked up several interestin' items."

Charlotte gasped, pressing her fingertips to her lips. "You've been to an adult bookstore? Do tell. I've always been curious as to what kind of books they would carry. I suppose a lot of D.H. Lawrence."

Eudora frowned, considering the comment for a moment. "I can't say that we saw any books," she replied. "They had a lovely selection of magazines, though. And the novelty items were quite interesting. But we were mainly there for the videos. We really needed to see what was new in the world of sex."

Eudora carefully refilled Charlotte's glass and tucked a fresh sprig of mint on the rim. "Things haven't changed much," she said. "The young people still enjoy the basics. Although, there did seem to be more of an emphasis on costumes. And we did notice that sex in public places was encouraged in these films. And it wasn't always just two people, if you know what I mean."

"There were animals?" Charlotte asked.

"Well, I suppose there may have been a few films

that featured horses," Eulalie said. "But I'm speakin' of other individuals. I believe they call them corgis."

"No, dear, that's the dog," Eudora said. "It's orgies. With an *O*."

Charlotte lowered her voice. "Speakin' of sex in public places, I remember when I saw Libby Parrish and Trey Marbury in the ladies' room at Tarrington's. I do believe they were about to have sex when I walked in."

"That was our first outside confirmation our plans had borne fruit," Eudora said. "I am surprised at how successful we were. I think we should try this again."

Eulalie shook her head. "Oh, I don't know, Dora. It was an interesting experiment, but perhaps we should stick to the more traditional methods of matchmaking. I'm not sure I could watch any more of those movies. The plots are just so silly."

"I don't think people really watch them for the stories," Eudora said. "With all that groanin', you can barely hear the dialogue anyway."

"Is that right?" Charlotte said with interest.

"We still have them," Eulalie said. "We wanted to throw them away, but Dora was afraid the garbage men would see them and think poorly of us." She took a sip of her tea. "Would you like to see them, Charlotte? The ladies won't be here for bridge club for at least fifteen minutes."

"Oh, I couldn't," Charlotte said. "Although, I must admit I am curious. You know, before my Harold passed, he was the only man I'd ever seen naked. I've always wondered whether he was…representative of the average male anatomy."

"I'm not sure you can gauge that from these films. It seems that rather than talented actors, they prefer to hire men who are extremely well-endowed," Eudora said. "I could get one of them up on the video player in Papa's study. Do you think the other ladies might be interested in watchin'? Believe me, when I first saw it, I have to admit to gettin' a bit hot and bothered by it all."

Eulalie took one last glance through the curtains and sighed. "You know, Dora, we do have one problem. Now that they're married, they won't provide any titillatin' new gossip. Perhaps that's reason enough to find ourselves another couple to turn our efforts toward."

"I'm sure the ladies of the bridge club would like to get involved," Charlotte said. "We could make it a club venture."

"It could be considered a community project," Eudora offered. "After all, Libby and Trey are gettin' married and they'll be startin' a family here in Belfort. And isn't that good for our community?"

The three ladies picked up their iced teas and walked back to the study, chatting about their newest project. For the first time in years, Belfort had become a most interesting place to live. And Eulalie and Eudora Throckmorton were determined to keep things that way for a long time to come.

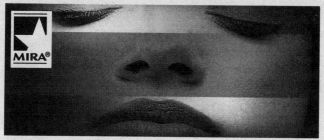

Receive a FREE hardcover book from

H A R L E Q U I N   R O M A N C E®

in September!

**Harlequin Romance celebrates the launch of
the line's new cover design by offering you
this exclusive offer valid only in September,
only in Harlequin Romance.**

To receive your
FREE HARDCOVER BOOK
written by bestselling author
Emilie Richards, send us four
proofs of purchase from any
September 2004 Harlequin
Romance books. Further details
and proofs of purchase can be
found in all September 2004
Harlequin Romance books.

*Must be postmarked
no later than October 31.*

**Don't forget to be one of the first
to pick up a copy of the new-look
Harlequin Romance novels in September!**

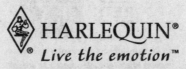

HARLEQUIN®

Live the emotion™

Visit us at www.eHarlequin.com

HRPOP0904

The world's bestselling romance series.

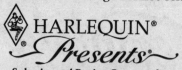

HARLEQUIN®
Presents

Seduction and Passion Guaranteed!

THEPRINCESSBRIDES

For duty, for money...for passion!

Discover a thrilling new trilogy from a rising star of Harlequin
Presents®, Jane Porter!

Meet the Royals...

Chantal, Nicolette and Joelle are members of the blue-blooded
Ducasse family. Step inside their sophisticated and glamorous
world and watch as these beautiful princesses find they have
to marry three international playboys—for duty, for money...
and definitely for passion!

Don't miss

THE SULTAN'S BOUGHT BRIDE (#2418)
September 2004

THE GREEK'S ROYAL MISTRESS (#2424)
October 2004

THE ITALIAN'S VIRGIN PRINCESS (#2430)
November 2004

**Pick up a Harlequin Presents® novel and you will enter a world
of spine-tingling passion and provocative, tantalizing romance!**

Available wherever Harlequin books are sold.

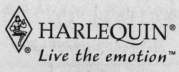

HARLEQUIN®
Live the emotion™

HARLEQUIN

Temptation

It's hot...and it's out of control!

**The days might be getting cooler...
but the nights are hotter than ever!**

Don't miss these bold, ultra-sexy books!

#988 HOT & BOTHERED
by KATE HOFFMANN
August 2004

#991 WICKEDLY HOT
by LESLIE KELLY
September 2004

#995 SEDUCE ME
by JILL SHALVIS
October 2004

#999 WE'VE GOT TONIGHT
by JACQUIE D'ALESSANDRO
November 2004

Don't miss this thrilling foursome!

www.eHarlequin.com

HTITF